Murder In a Blizzard

by Michael Lorinser

Copyright 2015 Michael Lorinser
All rights reserved

Published by eBookIt.com

ISBN-13: 978-1-4566-2584-9

This book is a work of fiction. All characters, places and incidents are fictional and are not intended to resemble actual persons, business establishments or localities.

No part of this book may be reproduced in any form or by any electronic or mechanical means including information storage and retrieval systems, without permission in writing from the author. The only exception is by a reviewer, who may quote short excerpts in a review.

To My Wife Karen,
For Her Continued Support and Understanding

And to All My Family and Friends
For Encouraging and Motivating Me

MURDER IN A BLIZZARD

Joey Norton charged into the newsroom. "Sorry I'm late. My car battery died overnight, and I had to wake up my neighbor to give me a ride to the auto supply store for a new one."

"Wouldn't be the first Saturday I've done the noon news without a producer," Austin said without looking up from his computer.

"I know. I know. Just another reason why they call you Awesome."

His fans had dubbed him Awesome Austin several years earlier, but the TV station did not change the name of his weekend reports to *The Awesome Austin News* until sixteen months ago. His unique ability to incorporate humor and personal insights into his broadcasts earned him a throng of loyal followers, numerous regional and national awards, and several job offers.

"The weekend is going to be a doozy," Austin said. "Last week we had our first January snow melt in over two decades and now we get this. Gets worse and worse with each alert."

"Each? How many have there been? I only heard the blizzard warning from the Weather Bureau."

"That was the first one. Strong winds and lots of snow coming into Minnesota from the Dakotas, starting this afternoon and lasting most of the day tomorrow. The second one came in an hour ago from the Minnesota Department of Transportation.

They are advising no travel throughout most of the state until Monday morning. If driving conditions get too bad due to the weather, MnDot will close some of the major highways."

"The forecast I heard was for feet, not inches, of snow, with winds gusting over forty miles-per-hour. Not many roads in Minnesota will be open if that happens."

"And roads won't be the only problem. Another warning came in within the last few minutes. This one from the Minnesota Communications Administration."

"That's a first," Norton said. "Let me read it."

The MCA is issuing a communications advisory for the northern two-thirds of the state beginning immediately. The severe weather and powerful winds forecasted for the area may cause local or widespread interruptions of most forms of communication. Outages may be intermittent or lengthy, depending on satellite reception and damage to lines and equipment. Service for landlines, cell phones, radios, televisions, and the Internet could be impacted.

"Guess you and I won't have to argue about what the lead story will be for your newscasts this weekend."

"You provide me with good film footage, even if it's from our files of other blizzards, and I'll do the rest. I'll emphasize the alerts and scare everyone into staying off the streets."

"And give the viewers some of your famous Awesome Austin pearls of wisdom."

"You betcha. I already have the first one."

"Lay it on me, bro."

"Woe unto those who do not heed my warnings."

* * * * *

Every April she ordered three new custom-made t-shirts. The colors varied, but the message printed in bold letters never changed. *I Don't Judge People*. The tradition sprung from her great awakening, a term she used to describe the month long period of soul searching that occurred two years after her divorce. The shirts were intended to remind her of the vow she had made to change her life for the better. She wore an *I Don't Judge People* t-shirt at least once a week during the summer months and occasionally under a sweatshirt in the winter.

For years Margarita believed she had been true to that vow. Sometimes she jokingly bragged about being the most nonjudgmental person in Minnesota, if not the entire United States. The fifty-something restaurant employee, who preferred to be called a waitress rather than a server, was not even troubled by the funky couple forced by the storm to spend the night dozing in booth number eight. The male's spiked hair, studded leather vest, and metal belt buckle the size of a DVD did not faze her. Neither did the female's silver lip ring, pink accented hair, and clothes in a kaleidoscope of clashing colors.

Now, as the paralyzing blizzard spilled into its second day, something was eating at her. No, not something. Someone. To her dismay, Margarita sensed the self-proclaimed most nonjudgmental person in Minnesota was on the verge of reverting to her old habit.

The uneasiness had begun the previous evening when a girl staggered into the restaurant toting a sleeping toddler. The girl in her late teens had to be, at least in Margarita's opinion, way too inexperienced to be driving in such wicked weather. Hadn't she heard the warnings to stay off the roads? She was lucky to have made it as far as she did without killing herself and the child.

Throughout the night Margarita could not resist the temptation to spy on the woman and the young boy who was with her. The nerves of all the motorists stranded over Saturday night at the truck stop's restaurant were on edge, but this woman appeared much more anxious than the others, frequently looking around the room as though searching for someone she needed to avoid. She had to be afraid of something. The behavior continued into Sunday morning.

A glint of a smile crossed the mysterious lady's face when Margarita appeared with an unordered platter of pancakes and sausage for breakfast. She asked the waitress about the weather report and the driving conditions. The response caused her to melt in dejection. Snowplows were pulled off the roads until after the storm. Most streets would soon be impassable, if they weren't already. MnDOT closed Highway 94 between Saint Cloud and Moorhead early in the morning. All major entrances to the thoroughfare were barricaded. As a result of the closing, no one would be able to leave the restaurant for several hours, and maybe not until the following day.

"We are all being held hostage by the blizzard," Margarita said.

"In that case, I better do something to keep my son entertained before he drives everybody crazy."

"Hasn't he been good so far?"

"Mainly because he's been asleep most of the time. I don't want to stretch my luck. Do you mind keeping an eye on him while I fight my way to the car for a few of his toys and books?"

"Not at all." Margarita peered down at the boy sitting on a booster chair scribbling with crayons on the back of a paper placemat. "It's not like this place is full of customers demanding attention."

"Thanks. I don't want to struggle putting him into his snowsuit just to go to the car."

The boy did not notice his mother slip away.

"It will only be a couple of minutes," she promised, her words muffled by the burst of wind crashing into the dining area as she opened the door leading to the parking area.

"Close that darn door," a male voice rumbled from a hidden corner of the restaurant, causing the woman to hasten her foray into the frigid whiteness.

"My name is Margarita." The waitress stooped low enough to be eye level with the boy. "What's yours?"

"Josh."

"That's a nice name."

"Do you know how to spell Josh?"

"No, I don't."

"J-O-S-H."

"You're a good speller, Josh. "How old are you?"

The boy raised four fingers on his right hand and used the pointer finger of the other hand to count them. "One, two, three, four."

"Are you really four?"

"Yes." He proved it by repeating the finger counting process.

Though Josh seemed to be about four, the woman accompanying him did not appear to be old enough to have a child of that age. Margarita jumped on the incongruity.

"Is that your mother who is with you?"

"No." Josh paused. "She's my mommy."

"Oh yes, your mommy." The waitress was still skeptical. "Where are the two of you going?"

"We're not going no place."

"I see. You must be coming from somewhere."

"We're not coming or going."

"What are you doing here then?"

"My mommy said we had to make a run for it."

Margarita stood speechless for a few seconds. Finally she whispered, "Were you running away?"

"I think so." His eyes drifted back to his coloring project. "My mommy said we had to run."

"Why?"

"I don't know." The whispering continued.

"Are you running from a person?"

"Maybe."

"Is it your daddy?"

"I don't have a daddy, only a mommy."

"Are you running because someone is chasing you?"

"I'm not running, silly. I'm drawing pictures. I runned here from the car with my blankie."

Josh resumed his art project, ignoring the waitress who continued to study him.

The restaurant's door banged open. The howling wind could not deaden the unmistakable cry of distress. "Oh, my God! Someone call 9-1-1. Please. Call 9-1-1."

* * * * *

The business district was completely deserted. All twenty-nine stores and restaurants were dark. Misty's Coffee and Bakery Delights was always filled with hungry customers every morning of the week, but not today. Misty's Delights was locked tight. Morning services and Sunday school programs were cancelled at every church in town. The towering street lamps remained illuminated beyond their normal shutoff time, but the wind-whipped snow obliterated the light they cast before it reached the ground. Everything was encased in white. A lone car labored down the street. Decals of a gold star and the phrase *Protect and Serve* adorned its side. Three inches of snow covered its roof.

The patrol car skidded to a halt a few inches from the orange and white post blocking the ramp to snow-covered Interstate 94. A door swung open and Deputy Justin Foneman plodded to the crank he had to turn to raise the barrier. The crank's icy iron handle stung his bare hands and sent a shiver through his body. He drove the SUV twenty feet forward and repeated the process, this time wearing gloves and lowering the post back across the roadway. Seconds later the car began edging down the sharp curve of the almost invisible road.

Over the years Deputy Foneman had come to despise two aspects of his job: notifying people of the death of a loved one, and responding to emergency calls during one of Minnesota's somewhat frequent blizzards.

The dreaded call had come over his crackling radio three minutes earlier, at exactly 9:09 on Sunday morning. "One down in the back parking lot of Midway Truck and Traveler Oasis." Kadence, the county dispatcher, always spoke in a monotone voice. "Unknown condition. Unknown circumstances."

Procedure dictated more than one responder be sent to such incidents. Foneman listened for Kadence to notify him another deputy or a rescue unit was on the way. His radio was silent. "Who's backing me up?" he finally asked.

"Working on it. We're short staffed because of the weather. The rookie is the only other deputy on duty right now, and he's at the other end of the county, more than an hour away from the Oasis if he can make it there at all. I've been in contact with state patrol dispatch. Their closest trooper may be further than that. They're still checking."

"How about an ambulance?"

"Problems there, too. Received word another one slid off the road a couple blocks from its garage. That's the second one out of commission. You may be on your own for a while."

"Wonderful. Keep me informed."

"Will try. Radio communication hasn't been the best."

Foneman cursed loudly as he strained to see the highway ahead. The wipers on his SUV were losing the struggle to keep the windshield clear of the falling and blowing snow. The speedometer indicated the deputy was moving at 15 miles-per-hour. At that rate, he would arrive at his destination in about fifty minutes. He dared not drive any faster.

"Near whiteout conditions on 94," he radioed the dispatcher. "Driving visibility is seventy-five to one hundred feet."

"Ten-four," Kadence replied.

"Be careful," a faint male voice added. "Don't kill yourself."

Foneman assumed the voice belonged to the rookie deputy assigned to patrol the northern part of the county.

"Believe me, I'm trying not to."

Justin Foneman had to try hard. Well over a foot of snow covered the highway. In some areas the wild wind created drifts almost three times that depth. Gusts of wind tore at his car, shaking and pushing it so hard that Foneman had to exert considerable force on the steering wheel to keep his squad on what he perceived to be the buried roadway ahead.

The deputy was grateful that Highway 94 was almost straight on the patch he was driving. He could recall only two short curves before he reached the truck stop with a person down in its parking lot. Foneman was also thankful for the new SUV the county had purchased the previous summer. Without its powerful four-wheel drive, he would quite likely end up stuck in the middle of a vast white wasteland. Only one tiny town appeared on the map between his current location and the truck stop. Wasn't much there this time of year. The whole town practically shut down when the summer tourists left.

Highway 94 had only been officially closed for six hours, but very few motorists had ventured out into the blizzard before that time. Foneman did not encounter a single vehicle as he slashed his way through the wintry nightmare, although he fully realized the blinding snow could be concealing cars or trucks that had inadvertently driven off the road. The thought had crossed his mind that he could be passing within a few feet of motorists trapped in disabled cars. He coerced himself to concentrate on his own driving.

Despite his slow pace, he feared a stranded vehicle would materialize out of the solid whiteness allowing him no time to avoid an impact. The red lights and siren on his sheriff's car were activated in what he knew was a futile attempt to prevent such an accident. The snow would certainly blot out the flashing lights, and the shrieking wind would mask the wail of the siren. Besides, how could a stuck car move out of his way? Nevertheless, the deputy wanted to do everything possible to not seriously injure himself a mere fourteen months and thirteen days before his retirement.

* * * * *

"He's closest to your semi trailer," Dontae Dakota shouted over the wind as he leaned over the fallen man blanketed with snow. "Do you know who he is?"

"Just because he's by my rig doesn't mean I know the guy." Marky's voice was tinged with a mixture of anger and sarcasm. He brushed the snow off the man's face. "Geez. I have seen this fella before. He was eating at the lunch counter last night. We barely talked. Never caught his name."

"What's he doing out here?"

"How should I know? Could have come out to get something from his truck."

"I thought you and me were the only truckers here. What's he doing in our parking lot?"

"Maybe he got lost in the blowing snow and couldn't find his way back in."

Tommy Glynn, the shift manager of the Midway Truck and Traveler Oasis who doubled as its most experienced cook, joined the two drivers. "Doesn't look good," the manager said after a quick assessment. "Is he dead?"

Marky stooped down to examine him more closely. "Not breathing." He felt the man's cheek and temple. "Ice cold. I'd say he's dead all right."

"Don't be so sure," Dakota said. "He may seem dead, but I've heard about people who look frozen but really aren't. You can't feel a pulse or see their chest move up and down, but they're not dead. Something to do with the cold slowing their metabolism."

"Either way, we can't leave him out here," Glynn said. "He'll be buried in two feet of snow and dead for sure by the time an ambulance gets here. We got to bring him inside."

"I don't know about that." Marky pulled up his jacket collar to cover his exposed neck. "I don't think we are supposed to move dead people until the cops come."

"We don't know if he's dead, and I'm not willing to leave him out here. It's too cold to argue about it. If you two burley guys don't pick him up, I'll carry him myself."

"I'll do it. But remember, if push comes to shove, I'm the one who said we shouldn't move him."

Slogging through deep snow always required effort, but the weight of the man the truckers carried combined with the windblown snow lashing at their faces made the eighty-yard trek to the restaurant especially challenging. Glynn shouted words of encouragement and counted down the remaining distance. He felt like a musher driving his team of huskies to the finish line of an

Alaskan dogsled race. All three were breathing heavily by the time they arrived at the door of the restaurant.

The young woman who had stumbled over the body sobbed as she huddled with her son and Margarita in the corner booth farthest from the door. The meager number of other restaurant patrons, all of whom had arrived several hours earlier, crowded around the rescuers bearing the limp form. Chevy Mato, a squeamish sixteen-year-old busboy and dishwasher, scampered to the nearby men's room. A scraggily older woman, who had been sitting by herself, placed her hand on the unfortunate man's face.

"What happened?" she said.

"Must have gone outside for some reason and got lost in the storm."

"Where should we put him?" Dontae Dakota's eyebrows were frosted white with snow.

"Take him through the kitchen," Glynn ordered. "We can put him on the big oak table in the food pantry. The rest of you stay here, unless you're a doctor or a nurse."

"How about a Catholic priest?"

"As long as you don't get in the way."

The priest followed them to the pantry, a small storeroom separated from the kitchen by a sturdy steel door.

The pantry walls were lined with shelves holding cans, bulky sacks, and boxes of foodstuff needed to operate a busy restaurant. A four-by-eight foot table filled the center of the room, leaving only a narrow aisle between it and the shelving.

"Okay, put him down," Glynn said after clearing a half dozen open containers from the table.

"What do you think?" Marky said peering at the body on the table. "Alive or dead?"

"Looks dead, but Dontae's right. It's hard to tell. He's cold, but he might still be alive."

"So we sit around and wait for him to sit up and thank us for saving his life?"

"Let's assume he's still living. We need to warm him up and get his blood flowing." Glynn adjusted the heat vent protruding from the wall so it would blow in the direction of the table. "Brush all the snow off him. Then unzip and open his ski jacket, but don't take it off. The lining will reflect the heat upward. Rub his hands gently. That might help with the blood flow."

The priest traced a cross with his thumb on the man's forehead and recited two short prayers.

Glynn disappeared into the kitchen, but returned a few minutes later with two folded dishcloths he had heated in the microwave. He placed one on the stranger's forehead and the other on his throat, and then he removed the man's boots and began to massage his sock-covered feet. "Anyone have other ideas how to warm him up?"

Glum faces and shaking heads were the only responses he received.

"I guess all we can do is wait and see if he comes around," Dakota said.

"I can do no more here," the priest said after a few minutes of silence. "He's in God's hands now. Do you mind if I take my leave? Some of the other folks might want to offer prayers for this poor fellow."

"Good idea," Glynn said to the departing priest. "He needs all the help he can get."

The three good Samaritans glued their attention to the motionless figure on the table, trying to spot even the smallest sign of life. At least one of them secretly hoped he would not see any, but a façade of concern and helpfulness had to be maintained.

* * * * *

Justin Foneman was the antithesis of the fictional law officers featured in movies and television dramas. He was not a flashy person. His graying hair was naturally messy, defying every gel or holding spray on the market. His teeth were gapped and a pair of cheap glasses framed his face on those spring and autumn days when allergies caused his contact lenses to irritate his eyes. A layer of belly flab protruded over his utility belt. In general, his appearance did not attract members of the opposite sex.

His normal patrol beat consisted mainly of farmland and a handful of Minnesota's famed 10,000 lakes. Lots of animals, both domesticated and wild, but few people. Almost as many tractors as cars. Only slightly more houses than boats. His duties were routine and far from heroic. No one ever shot at him, and he fired his own gun only once in the line of duty. He was aiming at the chest of a drunken deer hunter who had pointed a wobbly rifle in his direction. The bullet smashed into a metal *Private Property* sign a foot to the left and several inches above the head of the startled perpetrator, who, fortunately for both men, immediately dropped his firearm.

Foneman's IQ was slightly above average. His efforts to keep up with modern technologies produced mixed results. He was computer literate and could use many of his smart phone's functions, but his aging brain resisted learning the advanced elements of both. The same was true of the more recent developments in police equipment and criminal investigation. His inability or lack of motivation to retain such critical information was one of the reasons his tenure as a sergeant a few years earlier was short-lived. After a six-month trial period, he and Sheriff Schneider made a joint decision to terminate the experiment.

His annual performance reviews were always satisfactory. The only recurring negative remark by his superiors was his indecisiveness in situations that afforded him too much time to make a decision. He tended to over think the options and change his mind frequently. None of those occasions had ever been critical in nature.

Despite his shortcomings, Foneman was liked and valued by everyone in the department from the top on down. He had stellar work habits, was very reliable, readily filled in for sick or vacationing colleagues, and interfaced effectively with the public. A down-to-earth personality and a timely sense of humor helped defuse many disagreements and tense domestic situations. Off duty, his neighbors and fellow deputies could count on Justin to volunteer his help whenever it was needed. He was not above shoveling manure in a horse barn, babysitting an infant, or chauffeuring a senior citizen to a medical appointment.

His past achievements and the admiration of his peers were of zero value now. One hundred percent of his attention was needed to keep his car on Highway 94. The winter storm made seeing the road almost impossible. Less than twenty minutes into his mission the treacherous conditions began taking a toll on his body. His eyes watered from the strain. His tight grip on the steering wheel turned his knuckles white. Muscles stiffened in his neck, back and legs. Teeth clenched. The pounding in his head became louder.

Finally, he could no longer hold in the pain. He slammed his fist against the steering wheel while yelling, "Oh, how I hate this job!" A few deep breaths were followed by another smack of the wheel and a shouted, "Why does this crap always have to happen during every fricken snow storm?"

The tantrum lasted a total of fourteen seconds before the deputy forced himself to return to concentrating on his driving. He realized that any distraction whatsoever might have a disastrous result. While on other emergency calls he mentally prepared himself for the situation ahead and determined what he would do upon arriving at the scene. On this trip, however, he would need all his mental and physical energy just to make it to the scene.

Midway Truck and Traveler Oasis, or *the truck stop* as the locals called it, was not in Justin Foneman's patrol sector. All the same, he was very familiar with the establishment. He and his wife Stefanie had a habit of eating breakfast there before embarking on the tedious journey south to visit their three adult daughters who elected to remain in the Twin Cities after completing their college educations.

The Oasis was actually a small complex of attached buildings located on a lightly traveled county road that crossed over Interstate 94 in the middle of farm country. Exit ramps provided travelers easy access from both the north and the south. The dilapidated remnants of an independent gas station that went out of business years earlier still stood on the opposite side of 94. The nearest occupied structures were farmhouses located more than half a mile away in all four directions.

The complex consisted of two distinct areas for pumping gas, one exclusively for the giant tractor-trailer trucks that traversed across northwestern Minnesota, the other for all other gas users. Mechanics at the three-bay garage could perform minor vehicle repairs and maintenance while their owners shopped in a combination convenience store/gift shop or dined in the newly renovated restaurant famous for its home-style cooking. An elongated narrow section facing the massive truck parking lot in the rear of the building offered a coin-operated shower for truckers in need of such a convenience, as well as six closet-size sleeping rooms, each windowless and with just enough space for a single cot and a small bedside table.

Due in part to the blustery wind blowing unabated across the flat farm fields adjoining the highway, the snow was over a foot and a half deep by the time Deputy Foneman neared his destination. Thankfully, the same wind also blew most of the snow from the yellow sign with a thick black arrow curving to the left. Foneman didn't see the sign until it came within a foot of slashing the windows on the passenger side of his SUV. The car barely moved as he edged around the invisible curve. A huge sigh of relief signaled the driver's confidence that he was back on the straightaway and the truck stop was only a few hundred yards ahead.

"What the hay?" Foneman muttered to himself five minutes later. "Where the hell is the exit?" He barely could make out anything through the thick white veil created by the falling and blowing snow. The little terrain he could see looked exactly the same, flat and white.

"It's miserable out here," he radioed to Kadence after stopping his car. "I can't see a thing. The snow is blinding."

"What's your location?"

"I hope I'm still on the highway. Must be close to the Oasis, but I can't find the ramp going up there. For all I know, I could be in a cornfield."

"Hold on, I'll . . ." A ferocious wind squall blew across the tundra causing the remainder of Kadence's message to sink into static.

"Didn't copy," Foneman radioed back. "Say again."

Silence. The deputy repeated his message. Once, twice, three times.

A garbled male voice replaced the female dispatcher. "Where . . . GPS . . . you are."

"Can't copy," Foneman said. "Too much static."

"Use your GPS," the voice shouted back.

"I am. It only shows me as a stationary dot on 94."

Silently cursing his failure to master that function on his computer, Foneman poked at the touch screen attached by a flexible arm to the dashboard of his patrol car. After two failed attempts, he was able to enlarge the image of the map.

"This thing makes it look like I'm sitting at the restaurant's front door."

"You would be if you . . . the last ramp," Kadence responded. "I've . . . my tracker . . . about 600 feet past the exit."

"Okay, I'll try backing up. Tell me when I reach the exit ramp."

"No can do. Just . . .satellite . . . looks like . . . your own."

The patrol car began to creep backwards. Its siren masked the avalanche of swear words surging from the mouth of its only occupant.

* * * * *

Tommy Glynn sat on a folding chair next to the table in the food pantry. Except for *the guy*, as they had begun to call the poor fellow on the table, he was alone. The truckers had deserted him in favor of live companionship and the last of the raspberry sweet rolls Glynn had baked earlier in the morning. His eyes, heavy from the lack of sleep, fixated on the body.

The sound of shuffling feet interrupted Glynn's trance. He recognized the sixty-ish female approaching the open doorway as the same woman who had placed her hand on the lifeless man as he was carried into the restaurant. Like the others, she had spent the previous night at the truck stop.

"Do you mind if I come in?"

"Be my guest. It's kinda lonely in here."

"How's the guy doing?"

"He's not doing anything. Hasn't been since we brought him in. I think he's dead."

"Interesting."

Glynn thought the woman's response was a little odd. He watched her lean so close to the guy that their lips almost touched. Unsure of what to do or say, he introduced himself by name and connection to the restaurant. A response was quick to come.

"I'm Lannay," she said as she straightened up. "Lannay Sargetti."

"Sargetti? That's African, isn't it?"

"No, but you're not the first person to think so. It sounds too much like Serengeti. You know, that place in Africa with elephants and giraffes and other wild animals. Sargetti is as Italian as spaghetti. Lannay is a Hawaiian name. My mother always wanted to go to Hawaii. Then I came along unexpectedly. She couldn't afford both a trip and a baby, so she settled for giving me a Hawaiian name. I've been told she wasn't such a hot speller."

"Well, Lannay, whether your mother spelled your name correctly or not, you can pull up one of those collapsible chairs in the corner if you like."

Lannay Sargetti looked like an escapee from a prisoner of war camp. Faded clothing covered a frail body weighing ninety-five pounds at the most. Skin and bones would be an accurate description. Once alluring ebony eyes now sank deep into a wrinkled ashen face. Blood veins bulged from the backs of her hands. Dull gray hair, uncombed and unevenly cut, hung straight down to her shoulders.

She placed her chair on the opposite side of the table from Glynn. "I heard you don't know the guy's name," she said.

"We don't. He didn't have any identification. His wallet probably fell out of his pocket and is buried in the snow. You wouldn't happen to know who he is, would you?"

"Not really. He was at the lunch counter last night all by himself. Never saw him move from his stool or speak to anyone, although he did seem interested in that girl."

"Which girl?"

"The one that found his body. He was sneaking glimpses at her from time to time."

"She is a pretty good looker."

"Like me when I was younger." Sargetti didn't expect a response and didn't get one. After a lengthy pause she asked, "Do you believe in ghosts?"

"Ghosts?"

"Yes, ghosts. Spirits of dead people. I've believed in them all my life."

"Well, I don't."

"I've always wanted to be in a room when a person died. Feel his spirit leave his body. And now I'm here. I can feel his aura. It's sort of eerie, but calming. Can't you sense it?"

Glynn rolled his eyes, but before he could muster a response, Chevy Mato emerged in the doorway of the pantry.

"I think the cops are here!"

* * * * *

A sharp whoosh of wind announced Deputy Justin Foneman's entrance into the restaurant section of the Midway Truck and Traveler Oasis.

"It's about time," Dontae Dakota said with a smirk. "What took you so long?"

"Young man," the frazzled deputy said, "I spent more than an hour driving through hell to get here. For both our sakes, I suggest you keep your mouth shut until I ask you to open it."

The wind rushing through the open doorway propelled the menus off the nearby tall desk normally staffed by a hostess waiting to greet and seat customers. Taken aback by Foneman's words and tone, half of the restaurant's occupants stared silently at the floor.

"Okay," he said. "Who can show me where this person in the parking lot is?"

"He's not there anymore," Tommy Glynn said. "We brought him in. Hope that was the right thing to do. We didn't think it was good to leave him out in the cold and snow."

"Where is he now?"

"In the kitchen pantry."

Foneman brushed the snow from his boots and pant legs. "Take me to him."

As he followed Glynn and Marky, the deputy recognized Margarita as the waitress who had served him breakfast several times in the past. "Do me a favor," he said to her in a calm voice. "Call 9-1-1 and tell them I'm here. I radioed my arrival a couple of times from my car but didn't get a response, and my portable is nothing but static. It's the storm, you know."

"He stayed here last night," Glynn said as they entered the pantry. "Don't know when or why he went outside."

"What's his name?"

"Don't know that either. No wallet or anything with his name on it."

Foneman gave the guy on the table a quick exam. He could detect neither a pulse nor a heartbeat and saw no obvious injuries. The skin was cold to the touch, but that might not be unusual for someone who had been out in such frigid weather for who knows how long.

"What do you think?" said Marky.

"I'm no doctor, but this doesn't look good. I've got a set of paddles out in the squad. I'll give him a shock and see what happens."

"Shouldn't you wait until the medics get here to do that?" Glynn said.

"The medics aren't coming. No one else is coming. At least for some time. The ambulances are out of commission, and rescue trucks can't make it through this much snow. The other deputies are too far away. I'm all you get."

"I'm sure he's dead," Marky said after Foneman left the pantry.

The deputy returned carrying a narrow plastic suitcase. "My defibrillator," he said. "If this doesn't work, nothing will." He tossed his jacket, gloves and woolen cap into the corner. "Bare his chest while I get this gizmo hooked up. There's a scissors here if you need to cut his clothes."

Glynn spread apart the guy's well-worn cardigan sweater and unbuttoned and pulled apart his gray winter-weight shirt. "He's wearing an undershirt."

"Cut it."

Glynn made two snips with the scissor and stopped abruptly. "Geez Louise, I think this is blood." He pointed to a three-inch red oval on the side of the guy's white undershirt near his armpit.

Foneman nudged the truck stop manger aside and looked closely at the stain. "Looks like a blood stain alright. And there's more under him."

"Under him?" Glynn said. "How can that be?"

"Don't know, but I am not going to shock him until we find out. Let's roll him on his side."

"This is when I leave," Marky said as he was halfway out the door.

"Must not like blood," the deputy said. "You would be surprised at how many people faint when they see blood."

"You really want to move him?"

"No choice. We have to find where it's coming from, and if he's still bleeding we need to stop it. Move him very slowly and carefully."

"Shouldn't we take his ski jacket off first?"

"Not completely off. Let's take his right arm out of his jacket and sweater and top shirt so we can see things better when we roll him."

They extricated the arm and gently pushed the guy over on his left side. "Oh my God," the two men said in unplanned unison. The top third of the backside of the guy's undershirt was stained with coagulated, or perhaps frozen, blood. So was his gray top shirt.

Tommy Glynn's face paled. "I have to sit down."

"Take your time. I'm going to try to locate the source of the blood."

Within half a minute the deputy found the wound by pulling down the guy's shirts. A messy but discernable hole where the guy's neck was attached to his torso.

Glynn could tell by the expression on Justin Foneman's face that he had found something. "What is it?"

"Some kind of severe injury to his neck. Mr. Guy may have fallen on something sharp." Foneman stooped down to get a closer look at the wound. "Or he might have been shot. I think there are powder burns on his neck. The gun must have been close to his body."

"Suicide?"

"Almost impossible to shoot yourself in the back of the neck."

"You mean somebody killed him?"

"Can't say for certain."

"If not suicide what else could it be? An accident?"

"Of the three choices, I'd put my money on homicide. Like I said, I can't tell for sure."

"Homicide. That's absurd. Absolutely absurd. Who would do such a thing? Especially here at the Oasis? And in the middle of a blizzard?"

* * * * *

Deputy Foneman snapped photos of the corpse and the pantry's interior with his cell phone. He warned Tommy Glynn not to tell anyone about their discovery. "We don't want to panic anyone. If this is indeed a murder, the killer might do something to tip his hand."

"Or *her* hand." Glynn said.

"Or *her* hand. Whatever the case, let me do all the talking. I'll tell them the guy is dead. I'm sure of that now. But I won't say how, other than he might have frozen to death. We gotta keep everyone away from the body."

"Are we in any danger?"

"I hope not. I'm going to try to get more of my people down here as fast as possible."

"What do you want me to do?"

"Depends. Are you feeling better?"

"My stomach is all knotted up and my brain is racing a mile a minute, but other than that, I'm fine. I'll try to help in anyway I can."

"Good, you can do two things. As soon as we leave this room gather everyone into the restaurant. Staff and guests. And keep your eyes and ears open. Let me know if anyone says or does anything suspicious or out of the ordinary. Remember, mum's the word about how he died."

As he passed into the kitchen from the pantry, two distinct and pleasant aromas coaxed Foneman's mind to temporarily wander from the gruesome scene he had just left. The first emanated from the fresh coffee young Chevy Mato was brewing. The origin of the second, the tantalizing scent of warm cinnamon, was more difficult to trace.

"I put two trays of cinnamon buns in the oven," Margarita volunteered from the bank of stoves and ovens on the south wall of the kitchen. "Our guests already gobbled up your raspberry rolls and are getting hungry. The buns should be done in a minute or two."

"Look at that." Glynn said. "I'm away from the kitchen for a few minutes and they take over my job."

"Is he serious or joking?" Mato said to Margarita, who responded with a shrug of her shoulders.

Foneman shut the door leading to the pantry. "Any way to lock this?"

"Down here." Glynn pointed to a three-inch metal plate extending from the edge of the door in perfect alignment with a similar plate attached to the doorframe. Both had a quarter-size hole drilled through them. "A padlock fits in there."

"Get it."

"We don't have one. Never felt the need to lock the pantry."

"Do you have anything we can secure it with?"

"Not that I know of."

"I might." Chevy Mato had overheard the conversation. "I think I still have a bicycle lock in my locker." He returned a minute later carrying an eighteen-inch cable with a tri-tumbler combination lock at the end.

"Perfect," Foneman said. "Why do you keep something like this in your locker?"

"I can't afford a car so I sometimes ride a bike to work in the summer."

"Keeps you fit."

"I'd rather have a car."

After Tommy Glynn left to shepherd everyone into the dining area of the restaurant, Foneman threaded the cable through the holes in the metal plates and snapped the two ends of the lock together. "I hope you remember the combination."

"Of course," the teenager said. "One, zero, three."

"Don't under any circumstances tell anyone the combination. Do you understand?"

"Yes."

"And if you go into the pantry without my permission, you will spend the next five years of your life in jail."

"You don't have to worry about that. I have no desire to see a frozen man."

"Are you up for doing another favor for me?"

"Depends on what it is."

"Go out in both parking lots and write down the license plate number and model of every car and truck out there. If the truck has a company name or logo on it, write that down."

"Do I have to? It's colder than you know what out there."

"No, you don't. I only asked you because I don't know who else I could trust at this point."

Mato hesitated. "I suppose I could." His voice betrayed his lack of enthusiasm.

"Is there some way you can sneak out so no one sees you?"

"Yeah. That door on the wall with all the pans leads to a hallway and another door that goes outside. I'll have to prop it open so I can get back in."

"That's fine. Get going."

"But what if there's another body out there?"

"There won't be," Foneman said with a feigned certainty. He hadn't considered that possibility.

Margarita did not notice the teenager leaving as she entered the kitchen through the swinging doors. "I better take those cinnamon buns out of the oven before they burn."

Foneman nodded his consent and watched her use padded mittens to remove the trays of fragrant buns.

"By the way," she said. "I almost forgot to tell you. I got through to your office and told them you were here. They said to tell you your arrival time was 10:26, and they wanted you to call them as soon as you have a minute."

"It took me an hour and fifteen minutes to drive less than twenty miles." He struggled to pull his cell phone out of his pants pocket.

"You can try that thing if you want, but you're probably better off with a landline. I had to use it to call out because my cell phone was fading in and out. I don't know what's causing the havoc. The wind or the snow."

"Probably both. Where is the landline?"

"We have one line and four extensions. They all ring at the same time. One is over there by the refrigerators. One is in the convenience store, another in the fixit garage, and another at the hostess desk by the front of the restaurant. They are cordless, but you lose reception if you walk too far from the receiver."

Margarita began to spread a creamy white frosting on the buns.

"I'll use the phone in the garage. When you're finished with those buns take them to the folks waiting for me in the restaurant. Give them coffee or whatever else they want to drink. I'll be out in a few minutes."

"The door to the garage is locked. Tommy Glynn will have to open it for you."

* * * * *

Foneman dialed the non-emergency number to the sheriff's office. After six rings Kadence answered.

"I was trying to contact you on the radio," she said. "Are you free for another call."

"I turned the volume down so I can't hear it. The constant static from the unit on my shirt was driving me crazy."

"Are you available?"

"No."

"Are you sure? We are being asked to assist state patrol with a big mess."

"What kind of a mess?"

"Some fool of a truck driver in a hurry to deliver his load managed to get around the barriers on 94. Thought he could handle the snow. Three yahoos in cars decided to follow him. They didn't get very far. The semi jackknifed and all three cars crashed into it. They're in the north bound lane about ten miles south of your location."

"That's not even in our jurisdiction."

"I know, but the state patrol is asking us to send someone down to help out."

"Not me."

"Multiple injuries. Not sure how many or how bad. A farmer who lives on the highway is dragging them to his house on a sled towed behind his snowmobile. The patrol is requesting a state plow be sent up there."

"Can't leave here. I have my own problem. It's a big one."

"What's wrong?"

"The one down in the parking lot you sent me here for."

"Dead?"

"More then dead, maybe a homicide."

Silence.

"Are you there?" Foneman demanded.

"I'll try to contact Sheriff Schneider. He isn't due back from that conference in Milwaukee until tonight, although I'm betting he won't make it home until the blizzard is over. Sergeant Wyatt may be a better bet. Stay by the phone. Somebody will call you back."

The repair garage was chilly. The transparent plastic service doors, large enough to allow semi cabs to drive into the work bays, shook in the wind. Their rattling made Foneman feel colder than he really was. He searched in vain for a thermostat to turn up the heat. Rubbing his bare hands together didn't generate enough heat to justify the effort, so he decided to forsake the privacy of the garage for the warmth of the kitchen.

He sipped from a cup of hot coffee as he paced the kitchen floor waiting for the phone to ring. This was by far the greatest predicament he had ever faced in his entire life. A dead body in the food pantry a few feet away from him. A raging blizzard outside. A murderer potentially in the adjacent room. His boss out of town. And a slim chance of his law enforcement buddies arriving any time soon to help him.

Justin Foneman had never been involved in a homicide investigation, principally because the last murder in the sparsely populated county took place a month before he became a deputy. He had attended a few workshops about the subject, but the most recent was more than six years ago. He remembered about as much from those workshops as he did from the homicide investigation articles he had read. Very little. The majority of his knowledge came from the detective shows he and his wife watched on TV, most of which were fictionalized almost to the point of silliness.

The ringing phone startled him.

"Justin," a voice said. "This is Karen. Karen Lorenz."

Foneman felt an instant surge of relief. Karen Lorenz had only been associated with the sheriff's department for fourteen or fifteen months. She was semi retired, working sparingly for the three counties closest to her home on an as-needed basis, but she had loads of experience, first with the Minneapolis Police Department and then the Minnesota Bureau of Criminal Apprehension. As a senior detective with those agencies she worked only on major crimes, including numerous homicides.

"Tell me what's happening," she said.

The deputy gave her an accurate summary of what he had encountered since arriving at the truck stop.

"Sounds like you've done the right things so far." Lorenz's words did not match her thoughts. *Why in the world was he messing with the dead body? Looking for wounds should be left to the detectives or corner. Vital evidence has probably been contaminated.*

"You're going to come down here, aren't you?"

"Definitely. The question is when. The latest reports indicate the roads are impassable. Hard to believe it's possible, but the winds have become much worse over the last hour. They're blowing everything around. I can't even see the lake fifty feet from my patio door. The local fire department tried sending people out on snowmobiles for a medical call, a woman in labor, but they had to turn back because they couldn't see where they were going. Fortunately, it was false labor. You are the only one in the entire county who has been able to successfully respond to a call."

"Most of that was sheer luck."

"Sheer luck is better than no luck."

"How about a snow plow? I heard the state transportation people might be sending one of their big blades up to clear the way to a major accident south of my location. Can you get a snow plow to bring you here?"

"Never thought of that," Lorenz said. "It's worth a try. I'll have the dispatcher make some calls."

"What should I be doing?"

"For sure, the basics. Secure the scene. Don't let anyone in or out."

"I think Mother Nature has done that for me, at least until they open up the highway. Then we will have a problem. This is a popular place for people to stop on their way to or from the Twin Cities."

"I know. I've done it myself. Our troops will have priority. We will be on the scene before the highway barriers are removed."

"In the interim," Foneman said, "if some distressed motorist comes knocking at the door, I got to let him in. We'd have another dead body on our hands if I kept someone outside in this kind of weather."

"Of course, but limit his access to a small part of the building. In fact, do that for everyone who's there. We don't want to contaminate the scene any more than what's already happened."

"Done it. I have everybody waiting for me in the dining room."

"Fantastic. I'm sure you're already planning on getting their personal information."

"I am, and I have the busboy writing down the descriptions of all the vehicles in the parking lot."

"Assuming he can find them in the whiteout. What about suspects? Do you have any yet?"

"Nobody jumps out," Foneman said. "I've only talked to a few. I'll know in a few minutes exactly how many people are here."

"If there aren't a lot, you can start doing individual interviews. Find out what they know about the deceased, or, at least, what they are willing to admit they know. Make notes about their behavior during the questioning. Actually, record any thing that seems strange at any time, not just during the interview."

"Got it. Anything else?"

"Call the office with the information you receive about the cars. Have someone verify the owners and check for warrants and past criminal history. And, of course, be sure to preserve any physical evidence you may come across. Take a picture of it with your phone and try not to disturb it."

"I have a feeling most of the physical evidence is under about two feet of snow."

"You could be right about that. Any other questions before I let you get back to work?"

"None, except how quickly do you think you can get down here?"

"I'll call this same number when I get an answer about the snow plow. I'm also going to alert the state crime scene unit that we will need them ASAP, but don't count on them showing up until tomorrow."

"I'll be waiting."

"Well, Justin, I'm not terribly worried. I've heard so many good things about you. The sheriff and the other deputies speak highly of you. I am completely confident you can handle this sticky situation."

Detective Karen Lorenz's statements sounded contrived and were only partially true. She had heard many good things about Deputy Foneman, but she was worried. Despite his many years as a deputy, he had never worked a major crime scene. She was not at all confident he could manage the police work that needed to be done for a homicide at the Midway Truck and Traveler Oasis.

* * * * *

"That's all of them?" Justin Foneman asked Tommy Glynn as the two peered through the windows of the swinging doors leading from the kitchen to the dining area. "Only fifteen people out there and one of them is a toddler. You make sixteen. I was expecting a lot more."

"We're lucky. They'd be packed in here like teenagers at a concert if the storm had sneaked up on us. Everyone knew this one was coming. The Weather Bureau predicted the blizzard and MnDOT warned of hazardous driving conditions and road closures. Only daredevils, fools and the naïve come out in weather like this."

"What about staff? Is it only you, the waitress and the busboy?"

"Yeah, that's it. Hey, where's Chevy? Is he hiding some place again?"

"I gave him an assignment. He should be back soon. What about other employees? It takes more than three people to run this operation."

"Not during a blizzard. Margarita and Chevy volunteered to stay. I sent the rest of them home before the weather turned nasty. I called the others who were scheduled to work and told them not to come in."

"That must have made them happy."

"You bet it did," Glynn said. "No one wanted to drive in this junk, although one of our mechanics said he probably could make it if we needed him. He lives with his parents on a farm about a mile and half away."

The banging of the back door signaled the return of Chevy Mato, pink faced and teary eyed from the cold. "Here it is," he said between snivels.

Foneman took the pad of lined yellow paper and scanned the two pages covered with the teenager's notes. "You get all of them?"

"Think so. I couldn't see very far in front of me. Snow kept blowing into my eyes. I crisscrossed the parking lots until I bumped into something. We had a lot of semi trucks out there when the snow began, but now there are only two. One is unmarked. The other is from Double D Trucking in Michigan."

"Good man," Foneman said. "I'm going to call this into headquarters. You two can join the others. I'll be there in a couple of minutes. I owe you one, kid. Thanks a bunch."

"Does that mean I can drive without a license?"

"I don't owe you that much."

"How about a *Get Out of Jail Free* card?"

"I'll do better than that. I'll buy you the entire darn *Monopoly* game."

The kitchen phone rang before Foneman could dial a number. "I have a message for you, Justin," an office assistant at the sheriff's office said. "Detective Lorenz said the county is sending a snow plow to her house. She hopes to be with you in about an hour and a half."

"If you made it into the office today," Foneman said, "she should be able to do the same."

"Only if she stayed overnight at my mother's apartment in town as I did. I had to walk a whole block and a half, which wasn't as easy as it sounds."

Before hanging up he dictated the information Chevy Mato had gathered about the cars and trucks. The assistant said she would start researching it immediately and call him when she was done. She didn't anticipate it would take very long.

* * * * *

The restaurant at the Midway Truck and Traveler Oasis was open twenty-four hours a day and could seat 148 customers plus a few babies in highchairs. Booths lined the two walls of windows overlooking the automobile parking area and Highway 94. The twelve-person dining counter near the swinging doors to the kitchen was popular with over-the-road truckers fond of exchanging anecdotes with their peers. The remainder of the dining area was filled with tables of various sizes and wooden chairs with plastic cushions.

The room was cloaked in an unnatural silence even before Deputy Justin Foneman entered through the swinging doors. Four-year-old Josh slept on a booth bench. None of the adults had spoken much for the last five minutes.

Foneman introduced himself and asked everyone to move closer together so he would not have to strain his voice.

"The little boy sleeping in the booth can stay where he is, but I want the rest of you to sit at the tables so I can see you. Bring your beverages and sweet rolls or what ever else you may be munching on."

He scanned their faces, body shapes, and clothing as they followed his command. Although Lannay Sargetti's emaciated figure and old clothing stood out, he dismissed the elderly woman as harmless. Obvious differences existed between the generations, but even the young lady with the silver lip ring did not raise any concern. All appeared nervous or tense. Of course, who wouldn't under such circumstances?

"Alright, let's begin," Foneman said. "I want everyone to tell me four things. Their name. Where they came from. Where they are headed. And approximately what time they arrived at the truck stop. Any questions?"

"I have one," said Lannay Sargetti. "What can you tell us about that fellow we found outside in the snow?"

"I'm sorry to say the gentleman has passed away."

Sargetti waited for the chorus of groans and condolences to subside before she asked the obvious follow-up question. "How did he die?"

"I don't know that yet."

"Who is he?"

"Don't know that yet either. That's part of the reason why I will be asking all of you for a little information. Some publicly, some in private. Nothing to worry about. It's routine. Standard police procedure. Any other questions?" Foneman paused and looked around the room. "Okay, let's begin with the truck drivers."

"I'll go first. I'm Dontae Dakota. Usually when I give people my name they ask which one I come from, North or South Dakota. The answer is neither. I was born and raised in Montana and moved to Ann Arbor, Michigan some time ago. I'm hauling a load of replacement parts for cars from Detroit to Winnipeg. I pulled in here a little after midnight because my eyes were getting too tired trying to see the road through the snow."

Foneman wrote the essentials on the yellow notepad while intently watching the speaker. "Where in Montana?"

"The Billings area."

"You didn't hear the warnings about the blizzard?"

"I heard them, but I've driven through snow storms before. This one really got to me."

"Who's the other driver?"

"Me. My name is Marky. I'm from Devils Lake, North Dakota. I have a trailer full of five and ten pound bags of sugar. I picked up the load in Grand Forks early, thinking I could beat the storm to the giant grocery distribution center in Minneapolis. Instead I drove right into the heart of it. I decided to call it quits around 10:30 last night. Wasn't worth getting killed over."

"Is Marky your first or last name?"

"Sort of both."

"How could it be sort of both?"

"My first name was Mark, and my last name was, and still is, Key. As far back as I can remember everyone called me Marky, even my parents. My first wife somehow convinced me to legally change my first name to Marky. Officially, I'm Marky Key, but I only use Marky, except when I sign checks. My second wife likes the ring of it, so I never changed it back."

"Marky's good enough for me," Foneman said. "Who wants to go next?"

"I can," said the tall, thin man with a short haircut and dressed in black trousers and a black long-sleeved dress shirt. "I'm Thomas Pru. Father Thomas Pru."

"How many children did you father, Thomas Pru?" Dontae Dakota laughed at his own question.

"That's enough of that," Foneman bellowed. "I ask the questions here, and since I'm wearing the badge, I also make the rules. Rule number one is we *will* treat each other with respect. Understand?" He looked out at a sea of heads nodding in agreement. "Please continue, Father."

"I don't mind answering the question. Since I am a Catholic priest, I don't have any children. I followed Mr. Dakota into the parking lot. I nearly ran into him when he jumped from the cab of his big rig. At least, I think it was him. I could only see a blurry form through the snow."

"It was me alright. Wasn't expecting a car to be in the truck parking lot."

"I didn't realize there were separate parking lots until you informed me. In very colorful language I must say."

"So you arrived shortly after twelve?"

"I'm really not sure what time it was, but I thought it was earlier than that. I left Crookston after the Saturday evening mass and spent way too much time eating dinner and socializing with a group of friends in Moorhead. I should have stayed there. I was saying a lot of prayers the last twenty miles or so. I have a Monday morning meeting at the Saint Paul Archdiocese office."

"Your car is in the truck lot?" Chevy Mato asked in disbelief, while wondering how many other cars he could have missed.

"No. Thanks to Mr. Dakota, I realized my error and found the other one."

"Thank you, Father. Do you want us to address you as *Father*?"

"Whatever you are comfortable with. Father, Father Tom, Father Pru, or just Tom. All of them are fine."

Foneman pointed at the woman with the child. "Young lady will you be next?"

"Jade Byner from Minneapolis. My son's name is Josh. We are going to Manitoba to meet a friend. Stopped here for gas around 8:30 last night and decided to stay because the weather was getting so bad. I wish I had waited for the storm to pass before starting out."

"Short and sweet," said Foneman. So were the next seven.

Sharon and Jim Minder, an older couple traveling from Cottage Grove to Grand Forks to celebrate a friend's one hundredth birthday. Arrived around nine the previous night.

Allie and Jager Rellik, husband and wife in their early twenties returning to Minneapolis after spending their anniversary cross-country skiing in the northern part of the state. Arrived at 1:05 on Sunday morning. Had to rock their car out of snow drifts twice in the last three miles before they spotted the truck stop."

Ann and Larry Nussy escorting their adult daughter Kelly to their home in Maple Grove from her former fiance's house in the small town of Lake Bronson, Minnesota. Arrived at 11:10 p.m.

"Couldn't you have just said we were driving from Lake Bronson to Maple Grove without telling them my whole life story?" their crimson-faced daughter said aloud.

The only remaining guest was Lannay Sargetti. She stood so everyone could see and hear her. "I'm a ghost chaser," she proudly announced, causing heads to crank in her direction. "I'm on my way to the Palmer House Hotel in Sauk Centre. That's spelled with a R-E, by the way, not an E-R."

"We stopped at Sauk Centre once," Sharon Minder, a former English teacher, said. "Sinclair

Lewis was born there. He wrote books about Sauk Centre. *Main Street* is supposed to be the best."

"Yes, and Sinclair Lewis worked at the Palmer House as a bellhop. I hope you stayed there over night."

"No, we were on a tight schedule. Had to get home for work the next morning."

"Too bad. The hotel is haunted by the spirits of people who have died there. I hope to meet one."

"Good luck with that," Dakota said. "I'd say you only have a ghost of a chance."

Sargetti glared at her mocker. Her voice became louder. "I . . . have . . . supernatural . . . powers. I was in the pantry soon after that unfortunate man died." She continued to speak slowly, distinctly and in an eerie tone. "I could feel his spirit rising from his body. I still feel it now, not as strong as before, but I can feel it."

"Stop it!" Kelly Nussy shouted. "You're giving me the creeps."

Foneman moved to defuse the building animosity. "What time did you get to the Oasis, Ms. Sargetti?"

"Between 9:00 and 9:30. I felt like I was being summoned to this building. I knew why as soon as I came through the door. Someone was about to die here."

"Yeah, sure," Dakota said. "It's easy to predict things after they happen."

"Not after. Before the man died. Hours before." She paused to glare at a bright ceiling light. "Mark my words. All is not going to end well. One of you will soon be joining our deceased friend in the afterworld."

Sargetti's words, combined with her manner of delivery, left the others numb. Some stared at her as though they were hypnotized. Others fidgeted. Dakota forced an uneasy grin. Deputy Foneman wrote furiously on his notepad before fracturing the silence.

"Very interesting," he said. "And now for the staff. Mr. Glynn, how long have you been here?"

"Since eight Saturday morning. Working the whole time."

"Very admirable. And you Margarita?"

"Chevy and I ride together during the winter. Our shift started at three p.m. yesterday. I think we were about ten minutes early. We've been here ever since."

"Again, very admirable."

"I had to. Who would take care of these people if we left? Besides, I was afraid to drive home and figured I might as well earn a little extra money. I've been able to catch a few cat naps overnight."

Foneman rose from his chair, wetted his lips with his tongue, and waited until all eyes were upon him.

"Ladies and gentlemen," he said in an authoritative fashion. "Until I say otherwise, none of you are to leave this room."

"Why?" Dakota asked.

"Because I don't want anyone wandering around until I determine exactly what happened here. For you own safety."

"Can we go outside?"

"Why would you want to?"

"I don't know. Maybe to grab some fresh air."

"No, I want you all to stay in this room until the blizzard is over."

"What about the bathroom?" Sargetti said.

"If you need to use the facilities you must find another person of the same gender to accompany you. And you may only use the restrooms in the restaurant, not the ones in the convenience store or anywhere else in the building. The same holds true for food preparation. No person should be alone in the kitchen. I'm also going to be talking to each of you individually."

"What's going on here?" Ann Nussy's tone betrayed her irritation. "Can't go outside. Can't leave the room. We are being treated like common criminals. What did we do to deserve this?"

"Standard procedure when a person dies and we don't know the cause of death."

"Oh my God," her daughter Kelly shouted. "I bet the dead man was murdered! And you think one of us is his killer."

* * * * *

Attempts to diffuse the tension gripping the room fell flat. Foneman's reassertion that the cause of death was still undetermined went without challenge, but few in the audience believed it. The same was true of his explanation that it was normal to sequester people who were in the vicinity of such a death. Ann Nussy's accusatory questions combined with her daughter's retort swayed them to believe a murder could have been committed.

Half of his audience squirmed in their chairs. The other half sat as rigid as the giant statue in the Lincoln Memorial in Washington D.C. Foneman could see fear in some of their faces. Others looked perplexed. The priest appeared to be praying silently. Slowly, suspicious glances began to be exchanged from table to table. Except for a barely audible conversation at the Nussy table, the room was quiet.

Father Pru stood up. "I am very willing to stay together with everyone else, but may I first have permission to go to my room to get my Bible?"

"Room? What room?"

"We have six small sleeping rooms for the truckers in the back," Tommy Glynn said. "You passed them on the way to the maintenance garage to make your phone call. We divvy them out to truckers on a first-come-first-serve basis. One person per room. Fifteen dollars for up to eight hours. Another ten bucks for clean sheets."

"I have stuff back there, too," Marky said.

"Who else used one of those rooms?" Foneman asked. He wrote down the names of those who raised their hands: Lannay Sargetti, Dontae Dakota and Jade Byner. "That's a total of five people. Was one room empty?"

"No, the guy in the pantry had the last one," Margarita said. "He paid me for the sheets."

"Did you happen to get his name?"

"I only take their money, not their names."

49

"What about the rest of you? Where did you all sleep?"

"In the restaurant booths," Larry Nussy said. "For a little privacy."

"I'll escort the padre and Marky over to the sleeping rooms. Whoever else wants to retrieve their belongings can join us. But first I have a question, one I should have asked earlier. Do any of you know the name of the victim?"

His question received no response. His use of the word *victim*, however, did not go unnoticed. Assumptions were quietly made. The deputy must have been referring to a murder victim. The prospect of the dead guy being a victim of an accident garnered little consideration.

A pall of fear spread over the people stranded at the Midway Truck and Traveler Oasis.

* * * * *

The retirement home of Detective Karen Lorenz and her husband was modest in size when compared to some of the mini mansions gracing the same lake. The most enviable attribute of the house was a series of four floor-to-ceiling windows facing the water. The windows provided a captivating panorama of the lake and the abundant trees surrounding it. The views were spectacular, especially at sunset and in the autumn when the leaves burst into a blaze of fiery reds, oranges and yellows, although the four or five months each year the lake froze into one gigantic sheet of ice also provided an alluring, almost haunting picture.

The overwhelming negative feature of their house was the access to it. The sole way to get to it, other than on the water, was a gravel road so narrow that oncoming cars had to slow to a crawl to safely pass each other. Worse, the road tended to disappear after snowfalls of more than two or three inches, causing vehicles of unwary drivers to be towed from the marsh on the east side of the road.

"Can't be done," the detective's husband said as he removed his parka and boots. "The four-wheeler can't handle snow this deep. It just sinks. I can't get any traction."

"Did you try the lake? The ice should be plenty thick to support the two of us on a four-wheeler. We can take it to the public access."

"Same thing. Way too much snow on it. And the wind is blowing so hard on the lake you can't tell where you are. We could wander around in circles looking for the access without finding it or our way back home."

Karen squinted through one of the tall windows at the total whiteness engulfing her house. "I've arranged to meet the snowplow where our gravel road feeds into the county pavement, barely half a mile away. So how do I get there?"

Her husband pondered the dilemma as he warmed his hands over the burning logs in the fireplace. "Walking is out of the question. The drifts are too deep. We could borrow a snowmobile from one of our neighbors, but we would have the same problem with visibility. Any chance you can talk the plow driver into coming here? On second thought, I don't know how he's going to see through this white soup any better than we can."

"And he'd probably end up on the frozen swamp."

A ringing phone drew Karen to the kitchen. She returned a minute later. "It's a moot point. The snowplow got stuck a mile from the maintenance garage. They decided not to try to dislodge it until the storm subsides. Tonight at the earliest. More likely tomorrow, when it's daylight."

"That will be better for everyone concerned."

"Not for Deputy Foneman. And quite possibly not for me."

* * * * *

Justin Foneman commandeered the small business office adjacent to the hostess station near the front door. By changing the angle of the office desk to the door, he could sit behind it and monitor the movements of his charges in the restaurant. The accompanying side chair would be ideal for the personal interviews. The cordless phone from the hostess station worked perfectly in the office even with the door closed.

He had been unaware of the office until Tommy Glynn suggested he view the security cameras. Five of them monitored the exterior of the building including the two parking areas. A sixth watched over the cash register in the convenience store, and a seventh the register in the restaurant. The monitoring system for the cameras was hidden in a locked steel cabinet bolted to the back wall of the office.

Glynn showed him how to retrieve the images from each of the seven cameras for the last week. He demonstrated how to choose the camera and time frame he desired and how to stop, reverse, fast forward, or enlarge a portion of the image.

Foneman was ecstatic. The device operated much like his DVR controller at home. Within a few minutes he would be able to identify the villain who murdered the unlucky stiff on the table in the pantry.

Within ten minutes his glee had degenerated into disappointment. The exterior cameras were worthless. The heavy snow blotted out all activity in the parking lots for the last fifteen hours. The video from the camera in the convenience store was also of no value. Glynn had closed and locked the store at five o'clock the previous afternoon because there were no customers. The video from the restaurant was good solely for pinpointing the arrival time of each of the patrons. The lone person seen leaving after the murdered man arrived was Jade Byner on her way to her car to fetch her son's toys. Foneman resisted slapping the cabinet doors shut in frustration.

From behind the desk he studied the people in the dining area. Except for the toddler, he considered them all suspects, including the ghost lady. Based on appearance, they all looked like normal, law-abiding citizens seeking to ease their anxiety by immersing themselves in various activities. A few tried to nap. A couple others read. Some used their electronic devices to play games not requiring Internet access, which continued to function sporadically. The checkerboard, Parcheesi game and decks of cards Tommy Glynn had scrounged up were being put to good use. Entrancing soft rock tones of Jordyn, the latest female singing sensation, emanated from some unknown source.

Margarita's unexpected appearance interrupted his observation. The shadows beneath her baggy eyes were a consequence of her lack of sleep, but did not undermine the determined aura that surrounded her. She was a woman on a mission.

"I'd advise you to take a close look at Jake."

"Jake? Who's Jake?"

"That girl with the little kid."

"Jade. Her name is Jade."

"Doesn't matter what her name is. Something was not right between her and the dead man. He came in about ten minutes after she did and sat down at the dining counter. Tried out a couple different stools until he found one with a view of the booth where the girl was sitting with her sleeping boy. Ordered a chicken sandwich and fries. I never saw them talking, only glancing coyly at each other until she went to bed."

"Glancing? How? Like ogling?"

"No, I wouldn't call it ogling. More like spying. They were spying on each other. The few times their eyes met they both looked away quickly. The girl seemed scared. I asked her if she was okay, and she said no, how could she be okay when stuck overnight at a restaurant with a bunch of strangers."

"Was there anyone with her?"

"Only the boy. I think by choice."

"You mean she was a loner?'

"Yes. She distanced herself from the others. Except the priest. They had a five-minute conversation. I think it was about her son."

"How about the deceased. Did he have any contact with the priest?"

"Not that I'm aware of. Can I finish my story about the girl?"

"Please."

"This morning the little boy told me that he and his mommy were running away from something."

"Did he say what?"

"I asked. He said he didn't know. He also said he didn't have a daddy."

"Last night did Josh act like he knew the deceased?"

"Not at all. The little time he was awake he ignored the guy completely."

"How about the priest? Did the kid seem to know Father Pru?"

"Couldn't tell. He was down for the count by the time Pru got here."

"Interesting."

"One more thing, deputy. Five minutes after the girl and her son, if he really is her son, went back to those little sleeping rooms, the guy followed them. That is the last time I saw him until the truckers brought him in after the girl supposedly discovered him in the snow."

"Wow."

"Take it for what it's worth."

The conversation ended when the phone rang. The deputy escorted Margarita to the office door and closed it behind her.

"I tracked down some information for you about the owners of those vehicles," the sheriff's office assistant said.

"Anything of note?"

"Maybe. First of all, most of them don't have a record. Thomas Pru has a juvenile file but it's sealed and we can't get to it without a court order. The others have a smattering of traffic tickets, but that's all. Marky Key has the most. He was cited twice for driving his tractor trailer too long without taking a mandatory rest break and once for having an overweight load."

"No violent crimes or felonies in the bunch?"

"Maybe one. Dontae Dakota was arrested for simple assault and failure to obey a lawful command at that humongous motorcycle rally in Sturgis, South Dakota. Never went to trial because the charges were dropped. Doesn't say why."

"I can guess why. Years ago I grabbed a few extra bucks working security at the Sturgis rally. Minor assaults were not uncommon. We arrested bikers simply to get them off the street for a few hours so they could cool down or sober up. I heard many of them never made it to court."

"So much for accountability, but let's get back to my research. Want to hear something that will make your life easier?"

"Absolutely, I could use some good news right about now."

"I discovered you have some help down there."

"In what way?"

"A cop. One of them is a licensed peace officer."

"A cop? Which one?"

"Jon Silton."

"I'm not familiar with the name. He could be working undercover and using an alias. Can you give me a description?"

"I can do better than that. If your cell is working you should be receiving his driver license photo right about now."

Foneman did not expect to see anything on his phone's tiny screen, but slowly a fuzzy image emerged, barely clear enough for him to identify the man in the photo. "Holy shit," he said before expelling an elongated groan.

"Didn't go through? I'll try again later."

"No, I got it alright."

"So why the *holy shit*?"

"We got a dead cop on our hands."

The phone disconnected before the assistant could respond.

* * * * *

"We're sorry. All circuits are busy. Please try again later."

Justin Foneman banged the cordless phone on the desk after hearing the recorded message for the fourth time in the last eight minutes. He couldn't get through to either Karen Lorenz or the sheriff's office.

"I can't believe this is happening. I can't believe this is happening," he muttered over and over again, his face buried in his hands. How could a policeman be killed during a raging blizzard at a two-bit truck stop in the middle of nowhere? He realized he was losing the battle to remain true to one of the top commandments for all peace officers, namely, to stay calm in all situations.

The knock on the door jolted him. He wiped beads of perspiration from his brow, took a deep breath, and emitted an exasperated *come in.*

Marky opened the door. "I have a request," he said while standing before the deputy. "When you get around to interviewing people, I would like to be the first one on your list. I have something special to offer you."

"Do you know something about the dead person?"

"No, but I want to offer you my services."

Foneman was not in the mood to converse with anyone at the time. He responded with a tart, "I'll consider it."

"I think it would be to your advantage to . . . "

"I said I would consider it," interrupted Foneman.

Marky got the message. He sauntered from the office shaking his head and conjuring up reasons why the deputy had gruffly dismissed him without hearing his offer.

Foneman leaned back in the office chair and asked himself what other policemen would do in such a predicament. All of his ideas came from what he saw the make-believe cops do on television. None would work in real life. Especially when reality included a disabling blizzard.

* * * * *

Calls to Detective Lorenz and the sheriff's office continued to be answered by the same sterile-voiced recording. Foneman's frustration flared. He resisted the urge to hurl the uncooperative phone against the wall. "I have to stop feeling sorry for myself," he said aloud. "I can't let this crap get the better of me." He still didn't feel like talking to anyone, but he knew for the sake of his own sanity he had to find something useful to do.

Skirting the small crowd in the dining area, he marched into the kitchen. The aroma of cinnamon lingering in the air caused him to glimpse toward the oven in which the buns had been baked but did not slow his trek to the pantry. After assuring he was alone, he twisted the three tumblers on the blue bicycle lock to 3-0-1. The cable refused to separate. Perhaps the numbers were reversed. He tried 1-0-3. The cable popped apart.

Foneman slipped into the storeroom and closed the door behind him. Halting a few feet from the table, he focused on the dead policeman's face. The eyes were loosely shut. At first the mouth appeared to be closed, but a second look revealed a tiny slit separating the lips. The face bore no signs of trauma and did not appear to be that of a man who had suffered a violent death. Was it possible that he was shot after he had died from other causes? Or was Jon Silton alive for a while after he was shot and finally just gave up, closed his eyes, and passed away?

Foneman stepped nearer to the body, visually scanning it for any clue other than the neck wound that would indicate how the man met his demise. Nothing jumped out. The front of the body was free from blood. He didn't notice the scratches until he was taking a close look at the blood soaked into the right side of his undershirt. They were etched nearly vertically on the man's belt above his right hip. There were many of them bunched together within a two-inch space. Foneman knew exactly what caused the scratching because his own belt, the one he wore instead of a police utility belt when he was off duty, bore the same marks. The friction of a weighty weapon in a clip-on holster wreaks havoc on a leather belt.

"Well, Officer Jon Silton," he said to the dead man, "that begs the question, where is your holster and gun? For that matter, where is your badge? And your wallet and your keys?"

The deputy patted down Jon Silton's pants. Nothing, not even a Kleenex. His hands moved up the ski jacket. The pockets, both exterior and interior, were unzipped. And empty.

"Now where can they be?" Foneman pursed his lips as he thought. Two options. Either Silton removed the items himself or someone else relieved him of them. "Aha, I got it! The sleeping room. You were in one of the sleeping rooms. You emptied your pockets before going to sleep."

He left the pantry and hustled through the back door of the kitchen and down the corridor lined with the six small bedrooms. They were so sparsely furnished that searching them consumed almost no time. Look behind the door, under the cot, on the small table, shake out the sheets. Thirty seconds per room. And absolutely nothing for his work. Everything that had been in the rooms was removed, probably when he had allowed the occupants to recover their personal belongings. He should have paid more attention to who was removing what.

* * * * *

Justin Foneman's continued efforts to radio his office and complete phone calls on both his cell and the landline were miserable failures. He thought he was masking the uneasiness building inside of him as he stood in front of the assemblage of stranded motorists and restaurant employees. Unbeknownst to him, he was telegraphing the opposite by shifting his weight from foot to foot, tugging on his gun belt, and running his hand through his hair.

"Okay." he said in an unenthusiastic voice. "I'm going to begin the one-on-one interviews. I want to assure you that you have nothing to be afraid of. I'm not going to grill you like they do on television. I won't yell at you or push you up against a wall or threaten to send you to Guantanamo. We'll have a friendly conversation. If you would like, you can bring the beverage of your choice."

"I choose a tequila sunrise." Dontae Dakota's comment elicited a spattering of laughter.

"If you have one, you can bring it." More snickering. "This is what we are going to do. I'll take you one at a time to the little office by the front door. Bring your driver's license so I can make a copy of it on the machine in the office. I'll ask a few questions and when we're done talking I'll bring you back here. Then I'll take the next person."

"Can I bring my son?" Jade Byner asked.

"Better if you don't. He might distract us."

"I can watch him," Father Pru said. "I'll tell him another story. He liked the one I told him about the three kings following a star."

"Wonderful. I'll take someone else first, Ms. Byner, so you can prepare little Josh for your absence. Let's see, who should I choose?" He surveyed the room. "Marky, you're first."

* * * * *

Foneman left the door ajar. He wanted to be able to hear any commotion that might occur in the dining area. "Aha," he said as he perused Marky's North Dakota license. "You're the fellow from Devil's Lake."

"And take a lot of ribbing because of it."

With the exception of weightlifter size biceps bulging from under his shirt, the trucker was of average build and had a clean-cut appearance.

"Never been to Devil's Lake myself, but I hear it's a pretty nice area."

"Depends on how you define *nice*." Marky grimaced, grabbed his left arm, and pulled it against his side.

"Are you okay?"

"Yeah, just banged my funny bone against the armrest on the chair."

"Well then, let's get down to brass tacks. What time did you say you pulled in?"

"10:30ish."

"See anything unusual in the parking lot?"

"Last night? Are you kidding? All I could see was snow, and lots of it, blowing all over the place. Wasn't quite as bad as when we carried that guy in this morning, but close. Certainly not good for driving."

"When did you first see the deceased?"

"Right away. He was sitting on a stool at the luncheon counter. Playing with a few leftover French fries on his plate. I settled down next to him and ordered a slice of cherry pie with vanilla ice cream. Tried to strike up a conversation to pass the time, but he wanted nothing to do with it. Very standoffish."

"He must have said something."

"Yeah. Said he was on a job and needed to be thinking about his work."

"Did he say what kind of job or work?"

"No, and I didn't ask. I knew I wasn't wanted, so I just clammed up."

"Did you notice anything unusual about him?"

"Other than he didn't want to talk, nothing. I really didn't pay much attention to him. Like I said,

I know when I'm not wanted. I grabbed my pie alamode and moved to a table."

"Do you know someone named Jon Silton?"

"Can't say I ever heard the name."

After a series of questions produced only *don't know* responses, Foneman was ready to terminate the interview but felt the need to ask one final question. "I thought you said you had something special to offer?"

"I was waiting for you to ask. Should I tell you now?"

"Might as well."

"I think I can help you."

"Go on."

"I'm an author. I write mystery novels."

"Really? My wife may have read some of them. She's a mystery book junkie. Now that the kids are gone, that's her favorite pastime when I'm out on patrol. Reading mystery stories."

"I know she hasn't read any of mine."

"I wouldn't be too sure of that. She's gone through hundreds. Paperbacks, hardcovers, e-books. She reads them all."

"Not mine. I think my material is damn good. So do my friends. Unfortunately, literary agents and publishers disagree. All I get is rejection letters. The few who gave me a reason claimed my stories lacked realistic details. None of my books have ever hit the market."

"Tough luck, but I don't see how that helps me."

"I have an offer for you, one of those win-win situations. You let me assist with the investigation. I'll do anything you ask, take notes while you interview people, search the building, guard the body, be a snitch, anything. Who knows, maybe I'll find a clue you overlooked. In exchange, you fill me in on the details of the investigation. I'll use them in my next murder mystery."

"Murder? Who said it was murder?"

"You might be the only one in the whole place who hasn't said it. There was a lot of chatter about it after that mother-daughter dual planted the idea."

"Anyone say anything helpful?"

"No. Mostly rambling. People were anxious. It died away quickly, although I'm willing to wager the thought is still out there."

"I'm not a betting man. Besides, the odds are against me."

"See. I can help you out. Let me get involved in the investigation."

"Sorry, can't do it. Sharing details with a civilian is against department rules. Anyway, I'm not planning on doing much. A detective is on her way. She will do most of the investigating."

"She? A female detective?"

"Yes. She has a top notch reputation."

"How about a compromise? Don't give me any information, but let me do something to help. I'll look for details myself. If you like my work, put in a good word for me with the lady. Maybe she'll take up my offer or throw me some bones."

"Again the answer is no, but I'll keep your suggestion in mind."

"Sounds like a brush off to me. Another rejection."

"It is." He paused for a few seconds. "On the other hand, I just thought of something that may benefit both of us."

* * * * *

"Before I take Jade back to the office," Justin Foneman said, "I have an announcement to make." He waited until he had everyone's attention. "After I talk with each of you individually, I don't want you to discuss our conversation with anyone, including your own family members. Not one bit of it. If you do, you will be charged with obstruction of an investigation." Foneman didn't know if he could charge anyone with obstruction, but it sounded good. "I've asked Mr. Marky to be a monitor. He will report all violations to me."

Marky took a bow. "I'm not a tattletale by nature, but I take the deputy's request seriously. I hope I don't have to squeal on any of you."

Foneman thanked Marky and again told the others to relax because they had nothing to fear. He cautioned them about jumping to conclusions about how the man in the pantry died. No cause of death, official or otherwise, had yet been determined. Receiving no objections or questions, he motioned for Jade Byner to follow him to the business office.

"Nice boy you have," he said as he took her driver's license. "You must be proud."

"I am. He's a good kid. Likes to have fun."

"Are you his mother?"

"Of course I am."

Foneman's eyebrows curled. "You're twenty-one years old?"

"I am. And you don't have to say it. I know I don't look that old."

He studied the license for any irregularity indicating it was not genuine. The weight, height, and eye color listed on the plastic card matched the woman in the chair next to the desk. "Your hair is different. Did you dye it?"

"Doesn't every woman?"

"Is this your current address?"

"Yes, I live in Minneapolis."

"With your son?"

"Yes."

"Anyone else?"

"No." Byner sniveled. "Why are you asking me these questions? I didn't do anything wrong." A single tear leaked down her left cheek.

"I need to get some basic information about you."

"Well your questions are making me nervous. It's like you don't believe me."

"I'm sorry for that. Didn't want to sound accusatory. We can break for a minute or two if you would like."

"No, let's get it over with. I'll try to keep my composure."

"I'll be as gentle as I can. Let's talk about your employment. Do you have a job?"

"I'm a sniff specialist."

"Pardon me."

"A sniff specialist. At an expensive department store." Byner's face brightened. She relished talking about her profession. "I'm one of those ladies who dresses in a black smock and sprays perfume on female customers. My job is to convince them to buy one fragrance or another, preferably the more costly ones. My official title is scent consultant."

"May I ask what kind of money a scent consultant earns?"

"You may, and it's more than you think. The base hourly rate is barely above minimum wage, but the commissions are pretty good, actually more than pretty good, especially for the really expensive lines. And, of course, there's the occasional tip. Usually from a guy buying for his girl friend or wife. Women are lousy tippers."

"The store allows you to accept tips?"

"Yes and no. There's an official company policy against it, but management sort of looks the other way. I don't think they know how much we get when we smile, schmooze, and show a little cleavage. Mostly fives, but a fair number of tens and twenties. Twice I've been slipped a hundred dollar bill. Both times after I dyed my hair. Blonds may not have more fun, but they certainly get better tips."

"You report that as income to the IRS?"

"Am I supposed to?"

"I have no idea. I'm not a tax advisor or an IRS agent. Let's get back to something I do know about, like being a deputy sheriff. Was the deceased already at the restaurant when you arrived?"

"He might have been. I really don't know. I don't recall seeing him until twenty or thirty minutes later."

"Did he talk to you?"

"No, and I didn't try talking to him. He was sort of creeping me out."

"How so?"

"He kept looking in my direction all night long. Until I took Josh to one of those tiny bedrooms. I wasn't sure if he was peeking at me or Josh. I made sure the door was locked before I went to sleep. I put the table by the door as kind of an alarm. If he came through the door, the table would get knocked over and I would wake up. I didn't know he had an adjoining room until the waitress mentioned it this morning. Is he a rapist or a child molester?"

"Don't know much about him. Did you ever see him before last night?"

"No, I don't think so. He could have been a customer at one time or another. Definitely not a repeat customer or a big tipper. Or drop-dead handsome. Those are the ones I remember."

"Did you see him this morning?"

"If you count stumbling over him in the parking lot. Although he was so covered with snow I didn't know who he was until they got him inside."

"Did you hear any noises while you were in the sleeping room?"

"No, nothing. Josh was already zonked when I carried him in. I was exhausted, so I fell asleep almost right away."

"Did you see anything or anybody that looked suspicious since you arrived at the Oasis?"

"Only what I've already told you about the dead guy."

"On the personal side, you're not wearing a wedding ring."

"I'm not married and never have been. But Josh is my son. I'll show you my stretch marks to prove it."

"I'm sorry, but I have to ask another prying question. Where is Josh's father?"

"Honestly, I don't know. I was high on pot and the guy was passing through town. I never knew his name and never saw him again. That's the first and only time I've ever done anything like that. I'm really a good person and usually levelheaded, except for some bumpy times I went through after Josh was born."

"What kind of bumpy times?"

"Fought with my parents. I was living with them back then. Ran away from home for a few days. Everything is fine now."

"Does the name Jon Silton mean anything to you?"

Jade Byner hesitated. "Vaguely. I've heard it somewhere before. Or maybe it was Silson. He might have been on television. I can't remember. Am I supposed to know him?"

"Not necessarily, but please let me know if you recall anything about him."

"Of course. When do you think we can get back on the road?"

"This storm is supposed to last into the night, and then it will take time to clear the highway. I would say late morning at the earliest. You said you're on your way to Manitoba. Why are you headed up there?"

"Hope to meet up with a friend. This is the slowest time of the year for sniff specialists. The Christmas crush is over and the Valentine's panic won't begin for another few weeks. Nobody buys perfume between the two, unless they had a fight with their spouse or significant other."

* * * * *

"Dontae Dakota, do you want to come with me?"

"Do I have a choice?"

"Not unless you like wearing handcuffs."

Dakota was big and brawny, outweighed the deputy by sixty pounds and was three inches taller. A sturdy chain stretched from his oversized belt to one of his front pockets. A four-inch wide piece of thin red plastic dangled from a rear pocket. His black hair was straight and hung over his collar. His face was darkened by a four-day growth of stubble.

"You look like a biker?" Foneman said as he settled behind the desk, already aware of the other man's arrest at the South Dakota biker rally.

"Very perceptive. I do ride a Harley. Proud of it. Look at these tats." He rolled up his sleeves to reveal full-length tattoos covering both arms. "Beauties, aren't they? And I got more on my chest and shoulders. You need to have tats to run in a gang."

"Hell's Angels?"

"Nah, nothing like that, although we do look a little like the pictures I've seen of them and those other motorcycle gangsters. Leather chaps and jackets, head bandanas, whiskers, the whole works. The worst thing we do is get loud after we have a drink or two, might rev up our engines while driving down the highway. Old fogies get scared just looking at us. So do a lot of younger gals. It's a stitch. That's about as much harm as we cause."

"What time did you say you got here last night?"

"Technically it was this morning. Somewhere between midnight and quarter past. I was dead tired from fighting the snow. Didn't stay up long. I think I was the first one to glam onto a sleeping room."

"You work for Double D Trucking?"

"Not *work for*, I'm the boss man."

"Well, boss man, did you know the deceased?"

"Not until I saw him last night. He was the only one sitting at the counter. Everyone else was either at a table or a booth. I nodded but didn't speak to him. He sorta bobbed his head, very weakly, like a sissy. I was really tired."

"What was he doing?"

"Not much of anything. Fingering an empty glass, watching the others in the restaurant."

"Anyone in particular?"

"Maybe the two girls. The one with the kid and the one whose mom and dad broke up a bad scene with a fiancé. Actually, she was looking at him more than he was looking at her. Kind of staring. I didn't pay much attention to any of them. I went to bed."

"You slept in one of those little rooms?"

"I did. Not too many places have those any more. A lot of truck cabs have sleeping compartments now. But who wants to be crammed in one of those during a snow storm?"

"Did you hear any noises while you were there?"

"Not me. I was oblivious to the world. Slept for six hours. Got up to check on the weather. Saw it was still blizzarding and went back to bed for another hour and a half."

"See anything when you checked the weather?"

"Snow, only snow. I looked out the window on the back door. Didn't go up front to the restaurant. Not a creature was stirring, not even a mouse. At least in the trucker courtesy area."

"Did you see the dead man this morning?"

"Not alive. I helped carry him in, of course. I was almost sure he was dead from the start, but I convinced the others to try to warm him up, just in case, but he never twitched."

"What did you see when you went out to get him?"

"Same as before. Nothing but snow. In the air. On the ground. Snow upon snow. We had a hard time finding him at first. Couldn't see my white truck when we were forty feet from it. The girl who found him was trying to lead us but we got mixed up in the blowing snow and couldn't find him. She went in. Marky and I continued searching until we basically stumbled over him, just like the girl did the first time."

"Anything strange happen before or after finding the body?"

"Nothing."

"Have you ever heard of Jon Silton?"

"Of course. Sometimes on long hauls all I can get on my radio is country music. They play his songs over and over again. I prefer something more modern, like that new female singer. The one who uses only one name. Jordyn. Spelled with a Y. Yeah, she's the one I like. Jordyn. Real nice voice."

Foneman snatched up the jangling cordless phone on the desk. "Deputy Sheriff Foneman."

"Sorry, wrong number." Click. The anonymous caller hung up. Probably was calling on restaurant business and did not expect to have a deputy sheriff answer.

"The phone lines must be open. I need to make a few calls. Thank you for your help, Mr. Dakota. Let me know if you think of anything that could possibly be useful. Please close the door behind you."

"One thing before I leave. That nutty ghost lady is out there riling people up. She's telling anyone who will listen that another one of us is going to die before this blizzard is over."

* * * * *

" . . . candles."

"Hello, hello, this is Justin Foneman. What about candles?"

"Oh, Justin, please forgive me," Detective Karen Lorenz said. I was asking my husband to get the flashlights and candles out of the closet when the phone rang. The electricity has gone down in some of the rural areas. We want to be prepared if the same happens at our house. We don't have a generator like most of the farmers do."

"The Oasis better not lose electricity. The phones have already been a big headache. The landlines are finally working again."

"Everyone in the county and maybe most of northwestern Minnesota has phone problems. In between outages I've been able to make a couple calls on my cell. Still working on finding a way to get to the Oasis, but I did discover a few interesting things about Jon Silton. He was a cop in Sioux Ridge. His finger prints are being transmitted to our office."

"If I remember my geography correctly, Sioux Ridge is a fair distance south of here."

"Almost due south. I'm guessing three to four hundred miles. It's large enough to have it's own twelve officer police force."

"So what caused a police officer from Sioux Ridge to wander into our county during a raging blizzard?"

"I had the same question. I called the Chief of Police in Sioux Ridge, a fellow named Kevin Johansson. We had a twenty-minute conversation. Despite a lot of static and two disconnections, we were able to put together a few of the critical pieces of the puzzle."

"Better clue me in now before the line goes dead again."

"Silton's been with the Sioux Ridge Police Department for five years. They hired him right out of cop school. The first two years were shaky. He was written up a few times for improper judgment, but settled down after his wife had a baby girl who is now three. He still can be a little naïve. He's been recognized for his work with citizens and an employer group. No experience with major crimes because they don't have any in Sioux Ridge. By the way, his wife is pregnant again, maybe three months along."

"Damn."

"Yeah, my heart breaks for her."

"Did Johansson know his man was up here?"

"No, but that's the strange part. Three days ago Silton asked to take two weeks of vacation starting immediately. Said he might have to take some unpaid leave in the future. Thinking the pregnancy might be going haywire, Johansson asked if there was anything wrong. Silton said he had an opportunity to earn some big bucks on a temporary job, but was all hush-hush about it. Said he couldn't talk until after it was over. The chief knew the family needed money with the new baby on the way and wasn't terribly concerned about his officer taking on an outside job. He was confident Silton wouldn't do anything illegal."

"Did you give him the bad news?"

"I prepared him for the possibility. Told him we thought Silton's car might be one of several found at a truck stop and we are trying to match up vehicles with people. Also told him we have a body of an unidentified male who died from undetermined causes."

"How did he react to that?"

"As expected. Said he hoped the body wasn't Silton's and offered to help in anyway he could."

"I'm holding on to the same hope, although I'm ninety-five percent sure it's him."

"I'm taking your word for it. What's going on down there? Did you learn anything significant about your house guests?"

"Yeah, they all saw the dead man alive."

"Meaning they all had the opportunity to kill him."

"They did."

"What about motive?"

"Nothing even close to one."

* * * * *

His body language was a dead giveaway to Justin Foneman's exasperation with Lannay Sargetti. His rigid posture was accented by eyes frozen in an unwelcoming glare and a mouth clenched so tightly his lips were beginning to turn blue. The office chair was shoved as far away from the eccentric woman as possible.

Sargetti had responded to each of his questions with an elongated rambling about her experience with the spiritual world while completely ignoring the gist of what he was asking. She made clear her primary objective in life was to encounter a real ghost, not of the spooky variety, but a spirit who would reveal innumerable secrets about the afterworld to her.

The deputy sheriff resisted the urge to throw her out of the office and continued the painful interview. "What makes you think another person is going to die at the Oasis?" He was astounded by the relative brevity of her response.

"I can feel it. First in my bones and muscles." Lannay's words were labored. "Kind of a dull tingling. Then it goes to my brain. Sort of bounces around in there. No matter how hard I try, I can't make it stop. The result is inevitable. Someone is about to leave this earthly realm, someone I've seen in the last few hours. I'm always right. Always."

"Always? How many times has this happened?"

"Four."

"Tell me about them, but be brief. I still have to interview the others."

"The first was my grandma. She was only sixty-one and in good health. I had *the* feeling. Made me antsy. Didn't know what to do to get rid of it, so I walked a few blocks to a store to buy chocolate chip ice cream, grandma's favorite. When I returned I found her sprawled on the porch, dead from a heart attack.

'The second was a colleague whose cubicle was next to mine. All morning I had *that* feeling. He went out for lunch and never came back. Hit by a car while crossing the street. The third was a stranger who I talked to while in line to buy a ticket at a movie theater. She choked on popcorn during a gunfight scene in a Clint Eastwood western. They didn't discover her until the show was over. The fourth was last night. It was so strong I had a hard time getting to sleep. When I woke up this morning the feeling was almost gone."

"Could be a coincidence."

"Maybe once, but four times? The only four times I've ever had that feeling. Until you showed up. Now it's returned and getting stronger all the time. Number five must be on the way."

"You think it's some sort of ESP?"

"No, not extra sensory perception, although I have that, too. This is totally different. It takes over my entire body, not just my mind."

"Tell me exactly what you felt last night."

"I started getting that tingling as soon as I stepped through the door. It became stronger as the night went on. Like I said, I could barely get to sleep. When I woke up it wasn't very strong and went completely away after I sat next to the poor man they carried into the pantry. I could sense his spirit leaving his body. Could actually see vapor wisps floating up and disappearing in the air. I have supernatural powers, you know. I see things that are invisible to other people."

"You were there when the man died?"

"No, he was dead already. Ice cold. They let me sit by him soon after he died. Same as my grandma. I didn't see her pass. I only saw the vapors afterwards. I really want to be present when somebody dies. I wonder what..."

Lannay's wonderment was interrupted by a woman's scream, a male loudly questioning what was happening, and a second man proclaiming he had been shot.

* * * * *

Deputy Foneman pushed Lannay Sargetti to the floor behind the desk, ripped his Glock from its holster, and peeped through the five-inch slot created by the partially open door.

He was greeted by a chorus of crying, swearing, and loud voices. One person sprinted past Foneman's position in route to the restaurant's front door. Another followed. Other people were rushing in a muddled fashion into the kitchen or restrooms. The Nussy family was turning tables on their sides to create a mini fort. The cause of the panic was Mark Key, or Marky as he preferred to be called, who was heaped on the floor near the front door, grimacing in pain and clutching his left arm.

The deputy opened the door halfway but did not forsake the additional safety the tiny office afforded him. "What the hell is going on?" he roared.

"I've been shot," Marky yelled back, his voice filled with unmistaken anguish, as Father Pru and Tommy Glynn knelt at his side to provide aid.

"Who shot you?"

"Don't know," Marky moaned.

"No one in here," Tommy Glynn said. "He was outside when he was shot."

"Lock the door." Foneman shouted to Glynn while emerging from the office in a slight crouch, his Glock gripped in his hand and his eyes moving from side to side assessing the situation. "How bad is it?"

"My arm hurts like hell." He pointed to a bloody ragged hole in the left sleeve of his ski jacket. Another hole, smaller in diameter, was a few inches above the first. "I'll live," he groaned. "Can somebody help me get some of this stuff off?"

Father Pru obliged, first removing Marky's knit stocking cap and then gently pulling a leather glove from his left hand. The right hand was already bare.

"Can you walk?" Foneman said.

"I should be able to. My legs are okay."

"Good. We need to get away from the door and windows." He turned toward the gawkers creeping toward the wounded man. "Everyone go into the kitchen. Pull in a few tables and chairs from the restaurant on your way."

Pru helped Marky to his feet while Glynn began issuing loud orders to the others to assure compliance with the deputy's directive.

Foneman waited until he was alone before he peered through the partially frosted glass on the front door. Only thick sheets of blowing snow were visible. He crept to his right through an archway into a short corridor connecting the restaurant to the convenience store. The angle of the building partially sheltered the corridor's four windows from the wind. He positioned his face within an inch of the glass and strained to catch a glimpse of anything other than snow.

BAM!

The unexpected noise startled the deputy so much that his face flew forward, smashing with considerable force against the window. Ignoring the resulting pain and slightly blurred vision, he whirled around, his gun raised and pointed in the direction of the noise. A human form materialized near the office. His finger tensed on the weapon's trigger. His instincts told him not to shoot.

"I told you so," Lannay Sargetti screeched as she lurched past the hostess station. "I knew it. I knew it. Somebody tried to kill him. Didn't I tell you there was going to be another one? I told you so. I told you so. But you wouldn't listen."

"Damn," Foneman exhaled, grateful he had followed his instincts. "That was close."

He watched the hysterical woman hobble into the kitchen. The office door was closed. The earsplitting sound must have been caused by Sargetti slamming it shut. "Damn," he said again when he felt the blood dripping from his nose, embarrassed his own reflexes caused the injury. "I hate this job."

Foneman ripped a fistful of tissues from the box at the hostess desk and used them to blot the blood while slinking along the restaurant's two long walls of windows. Those on the north end were the worst. The vicious wind howling from that direction had coated the glass with a thick layer of snow. The entire exercise was in vain. Foneman could see nothing through the windows, not even his own squad car parked close to the building. He longed for the safety of his home and a nice warm bed with his wife Stefanie snuggled up beside him.

* * * * *

Justin Foneman holstered his Glock before shoving his way through the swinging doors leading to the kitchen clogged with tables and chairs procured from the dining area. He was greeted by a foreboding wall of silence from the assemblage huddled together near the bank of stoves and ovens. Not a whimper from the four-year-old boy held by Father Pru or another outburst from the ghost chaser. The absence of movement reflected a stark contrast to the wild flurry he had observed a few moments earlier.

All eyes were on the deputy. Fearful eyes. Questioning eyes. They were relying on him to be their savior. He quietly counted heads. Sixteen. Everyone accounted for. The presence of the entire group made the kitchen seem smaller. And smaller. And smaller. He could sense the pressure building inside his head. Now the room was slowly spinning, making him dizzy. He groped for the nearest chair, crumpled down on it, and slouched over the table in front of him.

"He's fainting," Sharon Minder screamed. "Do something!"

Foneman came close to passing out but did not. He buried his face in his hands and mumbled a few indiscernible words. Margarita hurried to his side with a glass of water, urging the deputy to sip its contents through a straw. Tommy Glynn grabbed the same cloth he had applied to the dead man's head, this time drenching it in cold water, and placing it on Foneman's forehead.

"Is he the one?" Lannay Sargetti intoned as she pointed at the deputy. "Is he the one who is going to die? Is he the doomed person?"

"Shut up," Dontae Dakota barked. "Shut up, you crazy bitch!" He pushed the offending woman back into her chair.

"I'm going to call for help," Margarita said.

"No, don't call anyone." Foneman's muttered words could barely be heard. "I'm getting better. Give me a few more minutes." He was correct. He soon showed signs of regaining his strength. "I didn't get any sleep last night and I missed breakfast this morning. Nothing like this has ever happened to me."

None of what Foneman said was true. Although his shift didn't begin until seven o'clock Sunday morning, he had reported to work twelve hours early because he feared he would not be able to make it to the sheriff's office once the increasing wind velocity fused with the already falling snow to generate a full-fledged blizzard. He slept for seven hours in a soft chair in the conference room, not comfortably, but he did sleep. Upon waking, he unpacked the breakfast Stefanie had prepared for him. Its contents reflected her campaign to force him to maintain a healthy diet: a single-serving-size box of raisins, a banana, a granola bar, and a peanut butter sandwich. He supplemented his wife's fare with two cartons of skim milk and a forbidden chocolate candy bar from the office vending machines.

The medical episode was not unprecedented either. He had experienced nine of them over the last few years. The first when his youngest daughter went off to college and the most recent a few months ago while arguing with his wife. None had ever happened while he was on duty. He never reported the occurrences to his doctor or his superiors in the sheriff's department.

Dontae Dakota approached the woozy Foneman from the rear. "Give me your gun," he said softly.

"What? No way."

"In case it hasn't sunk in yet, Markey was just shot. Someone out there is taking potshots at us, and you're in no condition to protect anyone, including yourself. I know my way around pistols. I've spent a lot of time shooting them at target ranges."

Foneman looked Dakota in the face. His weary eyes widened. "The gun stays with me. I'll use it on anyone who tries to take it from me. Now back off."

Dakota sulked away, surprised by the conviction and force of the response.

Margarita brought the deputy the last cinnamon bun and a tall glass of orange juice. She cut the bun into bite-size pieces and handed him the fork. He thanked her and slowly fed himself as a concerned audience watched his every bite.

* * * * *

Still feeling a trifle lightheaded, Justin Foneman bumped his way through the crowded kitchen to the table where Father Tom Pru and Marky were conversing. He pulled up a chair and pointed to Markey's bandaged arm. "Who's been doctoring you?"

"I have," Pru said before the other man could respond. "Had to cut the sleeve off his shirt. I stopped the bleeding and cleaned his wound. He was lucky. His arm was only grazed. Tore off some skin and nicked the muscle. I dressed it with some gauze from the kitchen's first aid kit."

"A doctor couldn't have done better. How are you doing, Mr. Marky?"

"Best I could be for having been shot. I'll live."

"Good to hear that, because I got a question for you. Why in the hell . . . pardon my language, Father . . . did you go outside? I told you to remain with the others. All of them were inside. You went out. Why?"

"I was doing you a favor. I thought I saw a light pass by the windows. Maybe a car moving around. I put my winter gear on and went out to investigate. Took two steps from the door. Heard the shot and felt the pain at the same time. Turned tail and came back inside."

"Was it a car?"

"Don't know. I couldn't see a thing, and have no idea where the shot came from or who fired it."

"Did you see the light?" Foneman asked Pru.

"No. I was sitting facing away from the windows. Marky was standing. Actually he was sort of strolling around the restaurant, watching the rest of us kill time. I saw him beeline for the door and throw on his jacket. At first I thought he had gone stir crazy and was making a run for it. I don't know if anyone else noticed him leaving until the cold air rushed in when he opened the door. The door was partially open when I heard a pop dulled by the wind and saw him stumble back in."

"So everyone saw him go out, get shot, and come back in?"

"Not sure about going out. Those who were in booths might have had their vision blocked. And I would imagine one or two might not have looked up from their reading or game playing or whatever they were doing at the time. After the door opened most of us saw him go out and tumble back in. Not the shooting though. The door was almost shut when he got hit, so we couldn't see that part of it."

"Who closed the door after he came back in?"

"Marky did, before he crumpled to the floor."

"Anything to add, Marky?"

"No, other than I was only trying to help you. Didn't think it was serious enough to interrupt your conference. I learned my lesson and won't do it again."

"All of us should have learned another lesson."

"What is that?"

"Somebody's out there with a gun. Somebody who is very willing to shoot whoever tries to leave. What we have to figure out is why."

* * * * *

Deputy Foneman slipped into the dining area of the restaurant, pointing his service pistol straight in front of him. He made a precursory search of the booths, primarily looking for adversaries secluded under the tables bolted to the floor. Finding none, he proceeded with caution toward the business office and was grateful to discover its door did not lock when Sargetti slammed it.

His short prayer was answered. The landline was still functioning. Detective Karen Lorenz answered her phone on the first ring. He updated her on what had transpired since their last conversation, but omitted his near fainting spell. In response to her inquiry about possible theories for the shootings at the Oasis, he admitted he had none, other than whoever killed Silton was probably still in the area because the blizzard had thwarted his escape.

Lorenz advised him that his primary responsibility was to protect the sixteen people at the restaurant. She cautioned him not to venture outside to hunt for the shooter. The warning was unnecessary. Foneman had no intention of going out in the blinding blizzard or staging a one-man search for an armed perpetrator. He very much wanted to be alive for his retirement in fourteen and a half months.

Lorenz summarized her efforts to get help to him as soon as possible. MnDOT agreed to send a snowplow to the sheriff's office as soon as it stopped snowing. It would cut a single path on Highway 94 all the way to the Midway Truck and Traveler Oasis, allowing reinforcements to access the scene.

"Now that I know you have an active shooter in your parking lot, I am going to request another plow do the same from the south. I'll beg other jurisdictions to send some of their officers behind it. We need all the help we can scrape up."

"How soon will that be?"

"I had been hearing sometime tonight, but a few minutes ago Awesome Austin, my favorite news guy, reported it might be earlier than originally predicted. But we still have one big problem to contend with."

"And that is?"

"We have to figure out how to get the deputies and myself over roads completely blocked with snow to meet the state plow at the sheriff's station."

A pang of depression hit Foneman when the phone call terminated a few minutes later. He was going to be on his own for several more hours, maybe overnight, and with a dangerous killer lurking somewhere nearby.

On his way to check the front door again, he spotted the oblong sign he had read on his visits to the truck stop with Stefanie. *Don't forget snacks and drinks for the road* – a large red arrow pointed to the right – *Available in our convenience store.*

"Nuts," Foneman said. He had been on his way to check the interior doors connecting the restaurant to the convenience store when Sargetti's noisy exit from the office caused his face to slam against the window. He had never finished the task.

The heavy double doors were not propped open as they always had been during his previous stops at the Oasis. A one-inch thick slide bolt held them together. The doors did not budge when the deputy pulled on the handles. "Solid bolt," he said to himself. "Nobody's coming in this way." For the first time since he left the comfort of the sheriff's office, a trace of a smile graced his lips.

His iota of euphoria was short lived, demolished by the realization that the bolt also had a darker, more negative aspect to it. It was on the restaurant side of the double doors. People could not enter the restaurant, which was good, but they could go out, which was not so good. A person, or persons, could have opened the bolt, passed through the convenience store, unlocked the store's front door, fired a shot at Marky, and in the confusion that followed, sneaked back into the restaurant and relocked the door.

The shooter may not be outside after all. He, or she, may be in the kitchen planning the next move.

*****

"I have to go the bathroom," Lannay Sargetti announced to Deputy Foneman.

"Well, you can't go into the restaurant. It's too dangerous out there with all those large glass windows. If the gunman brushes the snow off one of them, he could see every move we make. He may take another shot at somebody."

"What am I supposed to do? Hold it inside me until you catch the guy?"

"You have other restrooms, don't you?" The question was directed at Tommy Glynn.

"We have another set in the store."

"That's worse than using the ones in the restaurant."

"We do have one next to the sleeping rooms in the trucker courtesy area. A single stool and a sink and that's all. A little neglected, but usable. Were planning on remodeling it next month."

"Take me to it."

The tiny restroom could not have been more different from the spacious and well-equipped ones in the restaurant and convenience store. The walls begged for a fresh coat of paint, and the mirror above the sink was too permanently stained to reflect a clear image. Two exposed pipes stretched across the bare ceiling. An ancient wooden orange crate cowering in the corner contained extra rolls of paper towels and toilet paper. A cheap push-button lock on the door provided the only privacy the occupant could expect.

Adjacent to the dingy lavatory was a larger room housing a coin-operated shower stall. Beyond the shower room was an opaque door.

"That's the door to the garage where the mechanics work," Glynn said

"I know. You took me this way to make my first phone call. You had to open it for me. Is it always locked?"

"Always. For safety reasons. We don't want anyone wandering into the work bays and getting hurt. You need a key to go either direction, except when there's a fire. If an alarm or sprinkler goes off, it becomes an emergency exit and unlocks automatically."

"Who has the key?"

"Myself and the other managers, and there's one in the cash register for the mechanics to use when they run out of supplies in the garage. They have their own little lavatory back there."

"Who has access to the register?"

"Only the supervisor for each shift. The other mechanics need to ask for it. We have five supervisors and fourteen other men. Correction, twelve other men and two women."

"You have nineteen garage people?"

"To cover all shifts. Depending on the season and the time of day, we may have two, three or four of them working at a time. We're open twenty-four hours a day except for extenuating circumstance. Like a blizzard."

"Would the key be in the register now?"

"It was when I sent the mechanics home. I saw it when I took the money out."

Foneman glanced around. "What about the doors at the opposite end of the hallway past the sleeping rooms?"

"The one facing us is the storeroom. That's where we keep most of the stock for the store and garage and the non-foodstuff for the restaurant. Only the managers have a key. There's another entrance to the storeroom from a sliding overhead door on the loading dock. We only use it when we have deliveries. It only locks and unlocks from the inside."

"And the other door, the one adjacent to the storeroom, leads outside, correct?"

"Yes, it automatically locks when you shut it and can only be opened from the inside. Building codes require an unlocked emergency exit."

"Why does it have a window?"

"Good question, for which I have no answer. It's the only window in the courtesy area. That's what we call the sleeping rooms and shower we provide to the truckers, the courtesy area."

"Can we cover the window?"

"I'm sure I can find something to put over the glass, but why do you want it covered?"

"I have an idea," Foneman said, "but first show me what you keep in the storeroom."

* * * * *

"Okay," Justin Foneman said as he addressed his captive audience. "I know how cramped we all are in this kitchen. I'm sure I'm not the only one who's feeling a touch claustrophobic. So, for our own protection, we are going to build ourselves a little fort. And I do mean *we*, because I can't do it by myself. The fortification will help protect us from intruders and expand the space you can inhabit to include the six sleeping rooms, a not-so-state-of the-art lavatory, and the part of a storeroom not occupied by supplies. There is even a shower next to the lav if you want to freshen up."

"Hey," Ann Nussy said, "You're stealing our idea. You saw us making a fort out of tables in the restaurant when Marky was shot."

"You're right on both counts. I saw you and I'm stealing the idea. Except my fort . . . I mean our fort . . . is going to be bigger and better."

"Are all those places safe?" Sharon Minder said.

"Safer than you are right now in the kitchen. And much more comfortable. Although we do have one minor issue. All the doors will have to be barricaded from the inside. In case of fire, and I have no reason to believe we will have a fire, the barricades will have to be removed before we can exit the building."

"When are we going to do all this?" Sharon said.

"Right now. If everyone helps, we can be done in fifteen minutes or so. Because Mr. Marky's bum arm won't let him do much work, he'll help in the supervision of the project. And since the Nussys are such expert fort builders, any suggestions they can make during the construction process will be greatly appreciated. In fact, everyone's input is welcomed."

Foneman gave explicit instructions for what needed to be done, and the group set about accomplishing the tasks. Four people headed into the dining area with Foneman. The rest followed Tommy Glynn and Marky to the storeroom.

The deputy, his hand resting on the butt of his gun, stood guard as he watched his crew carry a half dozen of the six-person tables and several chairs from the dining room into the kitchen. They then flipped the tables on their sides and stacked them against the swinging doors. The tactic would not only slow down an entry into the kitchen, but would also serve as a crude alarm. Crawling over or moving the tables would create enough noise to alert the occupants of any attempted incursion or excursion. The concept was an expansion of Jade Byner's inspiration of placing a small table against the door of her sleeping room to alert her to intruders.

Glynn unlocked the storeroom, jabbed a triangular rubber stopper under the door to keep it open, and ordered his crew to carry its heaviest cartons down the hallway and pile them against the door leading to the maintenance garage. He asked Larry Nussy to duct tape a piece of plywood over the window on the door exiting to the truck parking lot and then had heavy boxes mounded against that door.

Marky's charges heaped the remaining cartons and other objects against the loading dock door and pushed the empty metal shelving to the rear, creating a large open space in the storeroom, which they quickly filled with the four-person tables and the accompanying chairs that had originally been moved into the kitchen after Marky was shot. The three small tables were left in the kitchen but shoved against a wall so they would be usable but out of the way.

Deputy Foneman inspected the work and made one adjustment. He propped open the single door that separated the kitchen from the back hallway with one of the smaller tables. He was satisfied the fortification, although not impenetrable, would provide at least some protection from the evil without. Now he could concentrate on the evil from within.

*****

"Thirteen adults," Foneman said. "Two people are missing. You all stay here. I'll go look for them. They couldn't have gone far."

He spied the missing men behind the almost closed storeroom door. Father Tom Pru and Marky were involved in an animated conversation about a jacket. "I need you to join the others for a brief meeting," he said.

"Now that we are all present," Foneman said to the crowd standing in the kitchen, "here are the new rules. First of all, under no circumstances whatsoever will anyone leave the secured area without my permission."

"Who would want to?" Sharon Minder said.

"Second, you can sit at the small tables in the kitchen or the larger ones in the storeroom and you can travel freely between the two, but please stay out of the way of the kitchen staff when they're working. Speaking of the kitchen staff working, it's after one o'clock. Tommy, do you think you could whip us up some lunch? The county will pick up the tab."

"Of course. I'll have a fantastic meal prepared in forty-five minutes. As long as the county is paying, I'll spare no expense."

"Appreciate it. Now to rule number three. If you want to catch a little nap or just be alone for a while, you can use one of those small sleeping rooms, but you must sign it out. I'll put a sheet of paper on the small table holding open the door between the kitchen and the hallway. Write your name, room number and your time in and out. Keep your door locked at all times."

Kelly Nussy raised her hand. "Can more than one person be in a room at the same time?"

"Sure, I won't stop you if you want to take a siesta with your mom and dad."

"Have you heard my dad snore?"

"No, and I don't think I want to. Let's move on to the fourth rule. Since people will be sleeping, try to keep the noise down. And I just thought of another rule. Numero five. We only have one bathroom for seventeen people, so try to limit your time in the john. Any questions?"

"How long do you think we are going to be cooped up like this?" Ann Nussy said.

"We are cooped up in here for two reasons. As far as the storm goes, it still looks like tomorrow morning will be the earliest the roads will be open. However, be advised we may delay your departure beyond that time. The perp who shot Marky could still be hanging around with another bullet in his gun. We won't declare the area safe until my colleagues thoroughly sweep it, and I don't mean with brooms."

"So we are being held hostage by both a blizzard and an armed desperado," Sharon Minder said.

"That's an accurate statement."

"Do you want to hear something funny?" Ann said. "Maybe not that funny, but certainly weird."

"Go for it," Dakota said.

"Years ago I went to London with my brother and his lovely wife and we saw a play at one of those famous old theaters. I can't remember the title of the play, but it had something to do with mice or maybe just one mouse. Everyone thought it was a big deal because a lady named Agatha somebody wrote it. Anyway, all the characters in the play were trapped in a small hotel during a blizzard. No phones or anything. One of them was a policeman, and someone got murdered. I think it was an old lady."

"If it was a British play, the butler did it," Sharon Minder said.

"Not in this one. There was no butler. I can't remember who did it. Might have been a man dressed like a woman. Oh wait, it was the cop! He killed the old lady and was trying to murder someone else." Ann glared at Foneman. "Nobody . . . suspected . . . the cop."

"Don't even think about it," the deputy snapped. "I wasn't here when it happened. Remember?"

"Or so you say," Ann said. "For all we know you might have been sitting out in the parking lot for hours before you came in. Come to think of it, the cop in the play was only pretending to be a cop. How do we know you are really . . ."

"Preposterous! Besides, I was with Miss Sargetti when Marky was shot."

"Does the word *accomplice* mean anything to you?"

"Don't even go there. I don't have time for that kind of nonsense. We are not talking about a fictional play or TV show. Does anyone have a sensible question?"

"Any more information about the dead man?" Dontae Dakota said.

"Not much. Pretty difficult to learn much of anything under these conditions."

"You asked me if I knew a Jon Silton," Marky said. "Is that his name?"

"Can't say for sure. There's a car in the parking lot registered to a Jon Silton from Sioux Ridge."

Now it was Jade Byner's turn to go pale and sway back and forth. "Are you okay?" Sharon Minder said. Dontae Dakota and the male Nussy reacted quickly to prevent her from falling.

"Mommy, mommy," Josh Byner whimpered.

Father Pru snatched up the little boy. "Mommy will be alright, Josh. She's just a little tired."

Josh reached for his mother. "Mommy, hold me." He began to cry.

Jade's eyes opened. "A chair," she murmured.

Jim Minder slid a chair behind her. Someone handed her a glass of water. Josh struggled to free himself from Pru's hold, while the adults watched his mother's gradual recovery.

"Josh," Jade Byner said after she regained some of her strength. Pru transferred the child to her. "Josh, I'm here. I'm okay." The boy snuggled up to his mother's chest.

Deputy Foneman stood over the whitish woman. "Do you need to lie down for a while?"

"That would be nice," she responded in a soft, tired tone. "The stress is getting to me."

"I'll watch Josh while you rest," Pru said.

"No, I want him with me."

"I'll have some of the women help you to one of the back rooms," Foneman said. "Remember to lock it." He cleared his throat. "Could I have your attention again," he said in a much louder voice. "What I said earlier still goes. If you see or hear anything suspicious, report it to me immediately."

"Or to me," Marky said.

"Or to Marky. He has agreed to continue to help me keep order and provide security. I'm confident we will all be just fine. Help is on the way and should arrive soon. We all know this is not the ideal situation, but let's make the best of it."

Once again, Deputy Justin Foneman did not believe his own words. And once again, neither did anyone else.

* * * * *

Four hundred and eighty-eight. That's how many steps Foneman took, beginning at the double doors with the tables stacked against them, to march through the kitchen and down the hallway with the sleeping rooms, check the door to the garage, make the u-turn back to the door with the covered window, walk into the storeroom, and return to his starting point.

After completing his most recent inspection tour, Foneman leaned against the wall and observed Tommy Glynn demonstrate food preparation techniques to Chevy Mato and Margarita, both of whom were given a one-day promotion to assistant chef. The clang of a falling pan from the opposite end of the kitchen interrupted the lesson.

"Sorry," Marky said as he retrieved the utensil that had fallen from a shelf of metal pans and bowls of various sizes. "Reading and walking at the same time is not one of my strengths." In his hand was a pad of yellow paper. The same pad that contained the deputy's investigation and interview notes.

"Give me that!" Foneman demanded as he rushed toward the truck driver. "What the heck are you doing?"

"Getting some paper for people to sign out sleeping rooms. You're the one who said we should do that."

"Where did you find that?"

"In that cupboard over there. I saw you put it in there. Once again I thought I was helping you, not committing a major crime."

"Did you read any of it?"

"The first few lines. I stopped when I realized what it was."

"Next time you want something from me, ask."

"In that case, Deputy Justin Foneman, may I please have several pieces of paper for myself?"

"What do you need paper for?"

"I want to write some things down for my next novel before I forget them. Where better to get realistic details for a mystery than at a real crime scene?"

Foneman ripped several pages from the bottom of the pad. Two for signing out rooms and the remainder for Marky. He waffled about accepting the man's explanation. On the surface Marky's excuse made sense. Yet, something about it gnawed at the deputy. Perhaps because he doubted Marky had stopped reading after a few lines. Or maybe because he realized he was at fault for not safe guarding his notes better. He poured himself a cup of coffee straight from the brewer, turned his chair away from the action in the kitchen, stared at the blank wall, and stewed over his uneasiness about the encounter.

The cup was almost empty before he looked down at the pad in his hand. He hoped reviewing the notes would snap him out of his funk. Fifteen minutes later he was convinced the drama unfolding at the Midway Truck and Traveler Oasis was one gigantic mess. Only a person with a lot more smarts than he possessed could unravel it. The exercise also reminded him of the three small family groups at the Oasis about which he knew next to nothing.

Jim and Sharon Minder seemed to be a harmless elderly couple. He could not picture either of them being capable of hurting another human being, let alone murdering one.

The Nussy family was a study in contrasts. Larry was reserved, easy going, and logical. His wife Ann, on the other hand, was excitable and at times irrational. Their daughter Kelly was by far the most fascinating of the three. Often amiable and levelheaded, but prone to short streaks of hysteria and callousness, proving she had inherited personality traits from both her parents.

Foneman had overheard her describing a former Italian lover, who apparently was one of several romantic encounters preceding her brief engagement to the now ex-fiancé. Kelly was on the rebound, and, very likely, on the prowl. Could she possibly be connected with the deceased officer? She was a year and a half younger, but so what? Both of them were attractive young people. Perhaps a little hanky-panky went on between them. But then again, he saw Kelly sidling up to the young priest. Father Pru was the same age as the dead cop. The deputy made a mental note to contact the authorities in Lake Bronson, the town in which she and her most recent boyfriend were living, to check if they had any information about the couple.

Allie and Jager Rellik were an interesting couple, or perhaps an uninteresting couple. Other than answering questions about arrival time and travel plans, they said almost nothing since the deputy arrived. Whenever possible they physically separated themselves from everyone else. They seldom communicated with each other, usually in hushed tones when they did. Most of their time was spent manipulating their touch-screen computers, although Allie had been observed drawing illustrations of fully clothed women on an artist's pad.

Foneman resolved to take a closer look at the Nussys and the Relliks. The three employees of the truck stop also required further scrutiny. One of them could have snuffed out Silton just as easily as a visitor. Jim and Sharon Minder fell to the bottom of his list of priorities.

* * * * *

Kelly Nussy almost collided with Justin Foneman while she was rushing to the restroom. Her puffy eyes and runny makeup suggested she had been crying.

"Are you okay?" the deputy inquired.

"No, I am not okay." Kelly used a tissue to dab away her last tear as her face wrinkled into a scowl. "Men are such jerks!" she screeched.

Foneman didn't know if the tirade was aimed at a former lover or one of the males at the Oasis. "Did somebody here hurt you?"

She hesitated several seconds before responding in a surprising soft, measured voice. "Not yet, but I'm scared to death he will."

"Who?"

"How should I know? Whoever is hurting people. He killed one person and wounded another. I don't want to be next. I want out of this place. I'm half ways to crazy."

Kelly's swift shift in emotions was curious. Within a second or two she had leapt from a teary and venomous condemnation of all men to a composed, mechanical and unconvincing declaration of her fear of being shot.

"What can I do to make you feel better?"

"Catch the guy who did it." She slammed the bathroom door shut. "And leave me alone."

"Women, women, women," Foneman mumbled as he resumed his patrol of the hallway.

The two older Nussys were playing cards with Dontae Dakota and Lannay Sargetti in the storeroom. None of them exhibited any real interest in the game. Dakota's right foot was planted on a long red plastic strip while he repeatedly stretched the opposite end up to his chest. Foneman surmised it was some form of resistance exercise and recognized the red strip as the material he had earlier seen dangling from the truck driver's pocket.

A few steps away Marky and Father Tom Pru occupied the table propping open the door between the kitchen and the hallway. The deputy could hear the priest talking about baptism, confession and penance.

"Trying to convert him to Catholicism, Father?" He said as he passed their table.

"Trying, but not succeeding. Marky's a hard fellow to convince."

"I'm the kind of man who feels he has to look out for himself and not rely on a god to do it for him," Marky said.

The Relliks sat at one of the small tables against the kitchen's rear wall. They did not look up as Foneman approached. Allie Rellik had shoulder length amber hair with pink highlights over each ear. A miniature silver ring jutted out of her lower lip. Her husband sported short spiked hair and a neatly trimmed half-inch beard, but no mustache. He wore a jet-black leather vest. All his clothing was various shades of black.

"Mind if I join you?" Foneman pulled up a chair, not waiting for an answer. "What are you up to?"

"Trying to design a new skirt," Allie said. "You like it?" She held up a drawing of a faceless mannequin wearing a skirt with almost a full-length ruffled slit up its side.

"Yes, I do. I would buy it for one of my daughters."

"Well, I hate it. It's the worst thing I've ever done. Who can concentrate on their work in this hellhole?"

"Scared?"

"Anxious. Tense. It's like we are sitting around here waiting for more bad things to happen."

"Do you have another option?"

"Nope. Like the lady said, we are hostages of the blizzard."

"How about you?" Foneman asked Jager. "How are you holding up?"

"This place sucks."

"Really, really sucks," clarified Allie.

"Count your blessings. What if you weren't able to push your car out of those snow drifts? The temperature is way below zero. You might be dead by now."

Chevy Mato tapped Foneman on the shoulder. "We're out of sugar. Mr. Glynn wants to know if you will get some out of the pantry?"

"There's no sugar anywhere else in the kitchen?"

"Not any more. We used it all up."

"Only in the pantry, huh?"

"Yep. In big brown bags on the middle shelf next to the door. One of them is open. You should fill this up." He handed the deputy a three-gallon plastic bucket.

"I'll be back," Foneman said to the Relliks. He was not thrilled to return to the pantry. Dead bodies always made him queasy, but this one was worse than the rest. More than likely, the corpse on the table was that of a fellow police officer. His stomach wretched. "There but for the grace of God go I," he told himself.

His idea was to go into the pantry, dump the sugar into the bucket, and get out in thirty seconds or less.

The plan derailed fast. "Oh, my lord," were the only words he could muster as he neared the pantry. His entire body tensed as he stood motionless in front of the door. The blue bicycle lock he had used to secure the room was gone! His mind whirled so fast he could not concentrate long enough to determine what his next step should be.

Finally, after almost a minute had passed, he conceived a plan. Nothing intricate, but enough to reduce the chances of being killed by someone hiding in the pantry. He glanced around the kitchen. No one was watching. Good, the more discreet he could be, the better. People were already frightened enough. And so was he.

He inserted a butter knife under the handle of the door to avoid smudging any fingerprints that might be on it. His right hand removed the Glock from his holster as he slowly pried the door open with the knife. He peeked into the pantry and exhaled a sigh of relief. No one, except the deceased man, was in sight. He inched his way inside. Then he saw it. The blue bicycle cable lock resting on the table next to the dead man's legs.

Foneman closed the door behind him and studied the surroundings. Nothing seemed out of place or disturbed since his last visit. Everything in the room, including the position of the corpse, matched the photos he had taken with his cell phone. So, why was the door unlocked and what had happened as a result of it?

Of all the characters at the truck stop, he asked himself, who would want to enter a pantry containing the dead body? Lannay Sargetti, the self-proclaimed ghost chaser, was the first to jump to mind. She had already expressed her desire to discover a way to communicate with Jon Silton's spirit. Anyone of the three restaurant employees might have had a need to fetch some sugar or other food commodity. But the most likely person had to be the killer. He, or she, may have wanted to remove a critical piece of evidence or plant a phony clue to disrupt the investigation.

Who had access to the pantry? In theory, only he and Chevy Mato knew the combination to the cable lock. The young busboy-dishwasher might have leaked that critical chunk of information to a third party. Or maybe some unknown person discovered a way to compromise the integrity of the lock and broke into the pantry. Or, Foneman hated to acknowledge, perhaps he had neglected to attach the bicycle lock to the metal plates on the door after his last visit.

The tumblers on the lock were set at 1-0-3, indicating whoever had entered the room knew the combination. So why wouldn't that person replace the lock on the door when he left? Did he forget? Did he intentionally leave it unsecured as some kind of message to the deputy? Or, for some reason, was he in a rush to leave?

"Shoot," Foneman muttered as he recalled the circumstances of his last departure from the pantry. He had been in a hurry to search the sleeping rooms for the slain officer's gun, holster, and identification. He remembered shutting the door, but had no recollection whatsoever of relocking it. The more he tried to reconstruct his actions, the more he was convinced he was the culprit. That conclusion raised more questions. How many people entered the pantry due to his negligence, and what did they do while they were in there?

* * * * *

The Relliks did not welcome Justin Foneman's return to their table. Responses to his questions were unemotional and terse. They volunteered no information about themselves or the case, but did reiterate their displeasure with the conditions at the truck stop. Their reticence led Foneman to suspect they were hiding something. He was about to confront them when Chevy Mato interrupted him again.

"Telephone call for you." Mato extended the truck stop's phone to the deputy. "A Detective Lorenz."

"This thing doesn't work in the sleeping rooms, does it?"

"I doubt it. You're better off staying in the kitchen."

Foneman retreated to an unoccupied corner of the room. He had already decided he would not mention the blunder with the bicycle lock to the detective. He spoke in a soft voice, hoping no one would overhear the conversation.

"Karen, I trust you're phoning to tell me you found a way to get here."

"No such luck, but I have made good progress in the case. Chief Johansson of the Sioux Ridge Police Department called me back about Officer Jon Silton. He talked to Silton's wife. Told her that he needed to get in touch with her husband and asked if she knew where he was or what he was doing."

"Let me guess. No to both the where and the what."

"Initially, yes. Until Johansson probed a little. She recalled that Jon had received several calls last week from one of the town leaders, an influential businessman with relatives on the city council. The two men had a long meeting the morning before her husband left town. Are you ready for the bombshell?"

"Can't wait."

"The businessman . . . his name is Byner. Harold Byner."

"And he's related to the Jade Byner here at the Oasis."

"Her father. Josh's grandfather. Chief Johansson has a history with Harold and Jade. Seems there was animosity between father and daughter beginning when Jade got pregnant and coming to a head a few weeks after Josh was born. Life was quite messy for the family, in part because Harold and his wife were habitual alcohol users, or perhaps alcohol abusers. Jade was a senior in high school at the time and wouldn't tell them who the kid's father was. After a particularly big dustup, Jade ran away from home with the baby. On the day before Christmas, no less. That was the year Christmas was so ungodly cold. Both she and the kid nearly froze to death. Actually they would have, if some old guys didn't find them. She returned home and the parents purportedly stopped drinking and everything was fine. At least that's how the story goes."

"Jade lied to me. She said she lived in Minneapolis and didn't know Silton."

"Maybe not. Johansson said Jade didn't want to become part of the accounting firm her parents owned so she moved to the big city to find a different line of work. That was about two years ago. As far as Silton goes, he participated in the search for Jade when she was missing, but there's a decent chance she may not have known him. After she returned from running away she became a model citizen. Was never involved with the law. Sioux Ridge is a small town, but not small enough for everybody to know everybody else."

"So it was just a coincidence they ended up here together?"

"The good chief had a sit down with Mr. Byner to ask the same question. Byner resisted coughing up any information, probably thought he was in trouble with Johansson. Eventually he admitted hiring Silton to follow and protect his daughter."

"Protect her from what?"

"Josh's father. Josh was conceived during a one nighter, or more like a one hourer. Jade hooked up with a stud older than her who was passing through town from Canada. Never knew his name. Never saw him again. Over the last year or so Jade became obsessed with learning the father's name and tracking him down. Byner and his wife were dead set against it. They heard through the grapevine that Jade received a strong lead about a fellow living in Canada. She was going to follow it up even though another woman living a mite south of the Minnesota-Canada border may have taken out a restraining order against the same man. They confronted Jade. An enormous battle ensued and Jade declared she was going to Canada despite the protests of her parents."

"That's when Officer Jon Silton entered the picture."

"Exactly. The parents didn't know where in Canada the baby's alleged father was living. They hired him to follow their daughter and learn as much about the guy as possible while watching over Jade and her son at the same time."

"Do you have the boyfriend's name?"

"Jade refused to tell them."

"Do you think they agreed to meet halfway, and he is one of the fellows down here with me right now?"

"Intriguing thought. It's a long shot, but anything's possible. The only info we have about him is that he's older than Jade. One way or another, we now have a suspect who had both the opportunity and a motive to take down Jon Silton. Keep a sharp eye on Miss Byner. And, if your theory is correct, we may have two. Jade and the man who fathered her son."

*****

The door to their sleeping room was locked from the inside. Deputy Foneman pressed his ear against the door when he heard voices coming from within. Unable to make out the words, he assumed Jade was talking to Josh or reading him a book.

The card game in the storeroom broke up amid good-natured taunts about cheating. Kelly Nussy twirled her hair while brooding alone in a corner, although Foneman noticed she was following the movements of Dontae Dakota out of the corner of her eye. Marky was at the small table in the hallway scribbling furiously on the paper the deputy had given him earlier.

"How's the writing going?" Foneman asked.

"Fantastic. I have a lot of great ideas for my new book. It will be about a man who gets murdered during a blizzard. Publishers won't be able to complain about its lack of realism."

"Who's going to be the villain in your great American novel?"

"I'm leaning toward an over-the-road truck driver, similar to that Dontae Dakota character. There's something strange about him. Maybe it's his split personality. He can be so nice at times, and then turn around and be sarcastic and mean. I wonder where he was when I was shot. He's certainly one of my suspects. What do you think?"

"Everyone is a suspect in my mind, including you."

"Me?" Marky's face brightened. "You could be on to something. What a great plot for a story. Mystery writer accused of murder. Then he gets shot. Survives to write a book about the experience. Non-fiction, of course. He will be the hero of the story, the one who captures the killer and gets the beautiful girl. Has to be a bestseller. Do I smell Pulitzer Prize?"

"Only if a Pulitzer smells like a cherry pie."

Foneman moved into the kitchen. "Is lunch about ready yet?"

"Perfect timing," Tommy Glynn said. "We have salad, bread sticks, two varieties of pasta and two kinds of sauces. A cherry dessert is in the oven and will be done in a few minutes."

"Sounds delicious. Where do you want the troops?"

"We will put dishes and food on the prep counter here. They can come in, help themselves, and carry it back to their tables. Chevy will bring around drinks."

The suggestion of food spurred the captives into motion. A footrace to the kitchen between Dontae Dakota and Kelly Nussy ended in a tie. Smiles were everywhere. Lunch provided a welcome reprieve from the last several hours of boredom blended with liberal amounts of anxiousness and downright fear.

"Do you know where Father Pru is?" Foneman asked Marky. "I wanted to ask him to say a short blessing."

"No, haven't seen him in a bit. Maybe he's catching a nap." Marky opted to scoop pasta and salad on his plate in lieu of volunteering to help search for the missing priest.

Foneman checked the lavatory and shower room for Pru. Nothing. With the exception of Jade

115

Byner's room, the entire sleeping section was also unoccupied. He rapped on her door.

"Yes?" the young woman said.

"Lunch is served in the kitchen. You better get yourself and Josh some food. I don't know when we will have the opportunity to eat again."

"I'll be out in a few minutes. Go ahead without me."

The deputy walked to the far end of the hallway, leaned against the wall, and waited for Byner to emerge. The door to her room opened slowly, inch by inch. A head popped out, facing away from Foneman. It retreated back into the room for a few seconds before a single adult figure appeared in the hall.

"Good afternoon, Father Pru," Foneman said. "We've been searching for you."

The priest took a few steps toward Foneman. "I was with Miss Byner," he said loud enough for Jade to hear his words so she could synchronize their stories. "She asked me to hear her confession and pray with her. She is very upset about what's been going on."

"Any sins I should be aware of?"

"You know I can't tell you that. The Catholic Church explicitly prohibits me from disclosing such things. What a person tells a priest in confession is privileged information protected by state and federal laws."

"I'm aware of that, but you have to admit it is a tad suspicious. A woman goes to confession on the same day one man dies and another is shot in the arm, and the priest won't reveal what she said to him. John Q. Public might believe someone is concealing something. Something pretty awful."

"John Q. Public may think so, but he would be wrong. My priestly vows won't allow me to divulge the sins she confessed to me, but I can assure you that Jade Byner did not kill or shoot anyone." Pru paused. "Now, since I've already said too much, I must respectfully terminate this discussion." He turned and walked toward the kitchen.

A minute later Byner exited the room holding her son's hand. She acknowledged the deputy's presence with a curt wave but exchanged no words with him. After she turned the corner into the kitchen Foneman searched her room. He found only a child's book and a Bible, the same nine-by-six inch one he had seen Pru reading earlier.

* * * * *

Justin Foneman sat alone dissecting his second piece of cherry cobbler. A first slice would not have been tolerated under his wife's healthy eating regiment. The guilt associated with violating Stefanie's wishes did not interfere with his contemplation about his next step at the homicide site. He concurred with Karen Lorenz's assertion that his primary responsibility was to protect the people at Midway Truck and Traveler Oasis, but he could think of nothing else he could do to achieve that end. He was content with waiting out the storm and letting Lorenz and the other county and state detectives do the investigating. The sooner he could get home to his wife the better.

Despite his best efforts, Foneman could not tune out the sounds emanating from the storeroom. Tom Pru was holding a post lunch prayer service. Only the deputy and the two Relliks had declined his invitation to attend. They were not immune from overhearing the prayers offered for the salvation of the dead man's soul and the fast healing of Marky's wound. A brief moment of silence to honor the deceased was followed by prayers for the peaceful capture of the perpetrator or perpetrators and a rapid and safe ending to their imprisonment at the truck stop.

The final *amen* had barely been uttered when a shrill scream erupted from the storeroom followed by the clanging of uprooted chairs and a cacophony of shouts and protests diminishing into the rustle of a swiftly moving mob. Foneman sprinted toward the clamor, poised to draw his gun at the slightest provocation. Allie and Jager Rellik, whether curious or frightened, followed close behind. They did not have to go far.

Dontae Dakota was dragging the puny and non-struggling Lannay Sargetti down the hallway clutched in a loose headlock. The crowd trailed them, spewing contradictory guidance to the muscular truck driver.

"Let her alone."

"Stop it."

"Teach her a lesson."

"Act like a Christian."

"Get her out of here."

"Shut her up."

"No need to be so rough."

"You big bully."

Justin Foneman exploded into the melee, grabbed Dakota by the collar and shoved him into the wall. "What the hell are you doing?"

Dakota did not relinquish his hold on the gurgling woman.

"She's at it again. Yakking about another person dying. Getting everyone upset."

"Let her go."

"But she's . . ."

"Release her. Now."

Dakota rolled his eyes before obeying. Sargetti drooped to the floor like a soggy towel.

"Listen up, folks." Foneman's ire could not be mistaken. "All our nerves are on end, but that's no reason to be going after each other. Dakota, if you pull another stunt like that, I'm going to snap the cuffs on you. And the same goes for the rest of you. I have two sets of handcuffs, and when they're gone I'll use rope. Keep your paws off each other."

"He assaulted her," Ann Nussy said as the group migrated back into the storeroom. "Why don't you arrest him?"

"No, don't," Sargetti stammered between short gasps for breath. "He didn't hurt me."

"As for you," Foneman aimed a menacing finger at the ghost chaser, "you will stop talking about spirits and making predictions about other people dying."

"But I can feel it. It's my duty to warn them. The spirits have given me the power."

"Enough of your babble! Do you want me to lock you up in a room by yourself? No one wants to listen to you carrying on like that."

"That's illegal. You can't lock me up. I have the right to free speech."

"I'm suspending your rights for the duration of your stay. Don't bother asking if I can do that. I not only can but I'm required to do it as part of my duty to keep control of a crime scene."

"A crime scene?" Ann Nussy rose to be face-to-face with the deputy. "Are you admitting that man in the pantry was murdered?"

"I didn't say anything about murder, so sit down." He waited for Ann to retake her seat. "This building is a crime scene because someone took a shot at Marky. Doesn't matter how bad he was hurt. Shooting at a person is still a crime. Aggravated assault at least."

The only sound that could be heard was Josh Byner's crying. The deputy's tirade had frightened him. The toddler's mother snuggled him in her arms and patted his back.

Foneman finally broke the silence, irritation still in his voice. "Let's all try to relax. We need to rise above what just happened. Blizzards don't last forever. The snow is going to stop. So will the wind. We'll be out of here soon. Just be patient."

*****

"Forty-five minutes of peace," Tommy Glynn said to Deputy Foneman. "Even the volume on

Kelly Nussy's music player is down a notch. The most noise I've heard is Chevy washing the pots and pans."

"I wish everything else was going as well."

"Such as?"

"The landlines are down again. All I get is a recorded message."

"I don't think that's ever happened before. Maybe because we've never had a bad storm last so long."

"What about Internet and cell phones? Are they always this way?"

"Remember we are out in the middle of nowhere. Internet service is always hit and miss. As for cell phones, the nearest cell tower is in White Moose Creek, and you know how far that is. We thought we were going to get one closer last summer, but the powers-to-be deleted it from the budget at the last second."

"Probably because none of them live around here," the deputy said.

"Not very many people do live around here, and that's the root of the problem. We aren't a high priority. Service can vary from one provider to another and from one day to another. The weather also can cause problems."

"Like today?"

Glynn snorted. "You got that right."

"Makes us all feel helpless. Bad enough being stuck in a blizzard, but being unable to communicate with the outside world makes it a hundred times worse. I'm surprised I haven't heard more grumbling about it."

"They've more or less accepted it. You're the only one who's asked to use the landline within the last few hours, certainly since we barricaded ourselves in. Maybe because there's not much privacy in the kitchen and our cordless phone doesn't work anywhere else. Last night a flurry of calls went out. We allowed brief calls on the landline when cell phone service began to peter out. From the little bit I overheard, it was basically telling family or friends they were safe and their cells were out of commission."

"Have you ever seen any of these people before?"

"If I have, I don't remember them. We have a hundred or two big rigs stop here every day and who knows how many cars. Once in a while I greet customers when I'm checking on the garage and convenience store, but ten minutes later they're erased from my memory forever. Most of my time is in the kitchen supervising the younger cooks and wait staff."

"How about Margarita and Chevy?"

"Both are good workers. Very dependable. They do things without being asked. Margarita has been a server for five or six years. She treats Chevy Mato like her own son. He started last summer when he turned sixteen. Never any problems with either of them."

"Are they related?"

"No, but they live close to each other. Maybe Margarita sees him as a substitute for her own son who she hasn't seen or spoken to since shortly after he graduated from high school. More than twelve years ago now. She's told me she looks over every young fella who comes into this place hoping to spot her boy someday."

"Do you know what caused the rift?"

"She never said. Actually, she doesn't talk very much at all about her past life. If you believe the gossips, the son's departure was somehow caused by her husband. They divorced less than a year after the kid took off. According to the grapevine, the kid might not be the husband's son. He was two-years old when they got married."

"What's Margarita's last name?"

"That's another thing she doesn't talk about. She avoids using it unless she absolutely has to. I know it because I see it on the payroll check I hand her every two weeks. It's Deville. Margarita Deville. That may or may not be her husband's last name."

"Margarita Deville. Sounds like an old song I used to sing to my wife."

"Could be the reason she doesn't use it."

"How about Chevy Mato?"

"Good kid. Likable. Dependable. Hard worker. They call him Vamp at school. He hates the nickname."

"Vamp? Like in vampire?"

"Yeah. I don't know the reason behind it. Doesn't look like one. Maybe he's a fan of vampire movies."

"I might consider looking into both Margarita and Chevy a little further. What about the Oasis? Ever have any legal trouble at the truck stop?"

"A few shoplifters and people driving away without paying for food or gas. Nothing serious. No robberies or murders."

"Until now."

Glynn licked his lips, "I guess there has to be a first time for everything, doesn't there?"

Deputy Foneman thanked Glynn for the cooperation and leadership he exhibited throughout the crisis and said he would mention his outstanding behavior to the owner of the establishment. He looked down at his watch. Time for another walkabout.

The Relliks were doing their usual thing, sitting in silence at the two-person table in the kitchen, staying as far away from the others as they could. They pretended not to see Foneman as he passed within a few inches of their table.

The doors on four of the six sleeping rooms were closed. The sign-out sheet indicated Larry Nussy, Dontae Dakota, Jim Minder and Chevy Mato occupied the rooms. With the exception of the female Rellik, all of the women including Margarita surrounded a table in the storeroom discussing TV reality shows, in particular debating how much of their content was staged. Josh Byner sprawled on the floor, quietly separating the red cards in a deck from the black ones.

Father Pru and Marky sat on cartons stacked against the entrance to the garage at the far end of the hallway. Although they conversed in low voices, Foneman was able to make out the words *jacket* and *sin*. They've been talking a lot about a jacket. Maybe Marky had swiped one and the priest was trying to convince him to confess the sin.

The deputy was relieved everything had settled down. He could sense his body was more relaxed, especially his neck and shoulders. He moseyed back to the kitchen and the last few bites of the cherry dessert on his plate.

* * * * *

Father Thomas Pru appeared to be making the rounds. He first attempted to engage the Relliks in conversation, but received the same cold reception afforded Deputy Foneman. He moved on to Lannay Sargetti, a much more receptive participant. Their dialogue soon disintegrated into a heated exchange about life after death. Foneman was about to intervene when the priest abruptly abandoned the ghost chaser in the midst of one of her lengthy rants.

Dontae Dakota was next. Within three minutes the truck driver snarled an expletive laced directive ordering Pru never to speak to him again and stomped toward the storeroom. Kelly Nussy witnessed the confrontation and approached the young priest. A civil discussion ensued but ended hastily when Nussy burst into tears.

Unscathed by his failures, Pru strolled into the kitchen in search of Chevy Mato. Instead, he found Margarita Deville. The waitress welcomed the priest with a broad smile and invited him to sit with her "for a spell." She offered him a fresh cup of coffee and homemade fudge from her secret stash. He accepted both.

The first few minutes of their discussion was composed of pleasant small talk. She spoke about her job at the Oasis and he described his education and pastoral experience. The conversation gradually became more serious. Smiles and relaxed eyes were replaced by rigid faces and glares. Margarita fought hard to keep her voice down so as not be overheard or attract attention. She was almost completely successful. Only Deputy Foneman was aware of the disagreement. Suddenly Margarita snatched the last piece of fudge from the plate and staggered away from the table while shielding her eyes with her forearm.

Foneman thought it was time to rein in the rebel rouser before he inflicted any more damage on the fragile tranquility of the truck stop. Pru was receptive to his lecture about doing nothing to disturb the delicate emotional stability of the trapped travelers and apologized for his actions.

"You and I need to talk about another subject," Pru said. "But not now. I need to organize my thoughts first. And I have a few commitments to keep."

"Let me save you some time. I've been a practicing Catholic for as long as I can remember."

Pru smiled. "No, nothing to do with religion, at least not directly. It's definitely something you need to hear, but I prefer it comes from another person, not me."

"About the dead man?"

"Him and others. We both must be patient. This has to be done in the manner that's best for everyone. I'm sure you will thank me later."

I've heard that line a hundred times before, Foneman thought, *and I've never wanted to thank a single person later.* He allowed the priest to escape without further challenge. However, he was curious if Pru's four antagonists would wish to disclose what had disturbed them.

He encountered Lannay Sargetti softly jabbering to herself as she paced up and down the hallway between the storeroom and the garage. Her otherwise blank face was dominated by two huge dark eyes staring zombie-like into nothingness. Not wanting to face the repercussions of disrupting the ghost chaser's trance, Foneman swerved into the storeroom.

One of the tables was filled with poker players striving to win a mother lode of pennies. A slight movement drew Foneman's attention to the barricaded loading dock door. There, almost completely hidden by the shadows and stacked boxes, lurked Dontae Dakota and Kelly Nussy. They were so involved in an intense whispered conversation that neither noticed the deputy positioned in the doorway. He feigned interest in the poker game while monitoring the secretive couple. He wondered if their conversation had anything to do with their encounters with Father Pru.

Jim Minder barged into the room. "Does anyone know where my wife is?"

"Check the sleeping room list," Foneman said. "Your name, not hers, was on it the last time I looked, but that was some time ago."

The exchange alerted Dakota and the young Nussy to the deputy's presence. Their awkward effort to transition from their hiding place to separate tables did not impress Foneman. Neither did Nussy's sudden interest in penny poker. He opted to delay questioning them. Instead, he pulled up a chair and kibitzed with the card players.

On his way back to the kitchen Foneman observed the priest writing in the upper and lower margins of his Bible. "Lucky my grandmother isn't here, Father. She once punished me really good for marking up my Bible. Called it sacrilegious."

Pru smiled. "My grandmother would have done the same. I only write in my Bible from time to time, usually thoughts or questions about the scripture I'm reading. Things I don't want to forget. Do you read the Bible often, deputy?"

"Not since the nuns forced me do it in Catholic grade school."

"I'm one of those people who believes the answers to everything are in the Bible. I often tell my parishioners to seek solace in the *Good Book* in time of distress, such as an unexpected death.

That's something for you to remember. The answers are in the Bible."

"Are you ready to have that talk yet, Father?"

"Naw, I'm still trying to get my head around it. And I'm awaiting a visit from an individual in need of my help."

"Jade Byner?"

"You should know better than to jump to conclusions."

"I should. Thank you for the reminder. Any other advice?"

"Be patient. It won't be much longer."

"I'm not planning on going any place. In fact, I'm sure I'll still be here long after you depart."

* * * * *

"Deputy, deputy." Chevy Mato jiggled Foneman's shoulder.

"I must have dozed off. How long have I been sleeping?"

"Beats me. I can't remember when I saw you last. Mr. Glynn told me to look for you. I found you slumped over and I thought something bad had happened, just like the wrinkly woman was predicting."

"Glynn wants to see me?"

"No, you have a call. He said it's the female detective. She's right here." Mato handed him the portable phone and disappeared into the other end of the kitchen.

"Justin," Karen Lorenz said, "I have lots of good news. The snow has stopped at my house and the phones are back up. I was able to make some calls and we have an action plan."

"I hope the plan is for you to be here in five minutes."

"Not that soon, but we are coming. From two directions. Four of us, two deputies, a state trooper and me behind a plow from the north. Eight or nine cops from various agencies coming behind a plow from the south."

"When?"

"Not exactly sure. The wind is still blowing everything around, but the visibility is much improved now that the snow has stopped. The county boys have to bring us to the sheriff's office to meet the state plow. They think they can get a local plow to my house within an hour. A neighbor is lending me her snowshoes so I can walk to the county road. After that, it all depends on how bad the interstate is. We're shooting for an arrival between seven and seven-thirty."

"Tonight, not tomorrow morning, right?"

"Of course. We're going to coordinate our arrival. The first plow to get close will stop about a mile from your site and wait for the other one. When both are a mile away we will converge on your location."

"What do you want me to do?"

"Just hold tight. Keep everyone safe. We'll let you know when we get there."

"What about the guy who shot Marky?"

"That's the reason for coming in force. If he's still there, and still alive, we are hoping he sees he's outnumbered and gives himself up. If not, we'll search every car and every truck and every place somebody could be hiding around the building."

"He could be in the repair garage or the convenience store or the main part of the restaurant."

"We'll search those, too, even if we find somebody outside. As the saying goes, no stone will be left unturned. Can we get into the store and the garage from the outside or do we have to come through the restaurant?"

"Yes and no. They both have exterior doors but they are locked, so is the entrance to the restaurant for that matter. Once you get inside the restaurant, you have interior access to the store and the garage."

"So what do you suggest?"

"Try calling me when you're here and I'll unlock the restaurant. If you can't get through to me, bang on the front door."

"If that doesn't work?"

"Break it down."

"We'll do whatever we have to do. We *will* find him wherever he is hiding."

"I know, but we shouldn't lose sight of the other possibility."

"Which is?"

"He may not be hiding. He may be part of the group I'm trying to protect."

* * * * *

Lorenz had warned Deputy Foneman not to divulge the details of the plan to his fellow captives. She did say, however, he could reveal the approximate timing of the event, but only if he thought it served a useful purpose.

Foneman weighed the pros and cons of such an announcement. Would the knowledge of the pending arrival of more officers comfort the group because they would feel more secure and know the end to the ordeal was near? Or would it cause more anxiety over what might transpire before and after the cops show up? A second opinion from someone close to the issue would be useful.

Tommy Glynn listened to Foneman describe the two sides of the argument. He agreed the decision was difficult because both proposals had merit. After several seconds of silent thought he voted to disclose the information. Any bit of good news would be welcome.

Piggybacking on his own recommendation, Glynn suggested turning the announcement into a small celebration. He could put birthday candles into pre-made cupcakes and serve them with ice cream. Foneman agreed that the surprise might improve everybody's mood. Lunch certainly had a positive impact. Fortunately, Stefanie wasn't there to condemn the serving of another calorie-laden treat.

Fifteen minutes later Foneman summoned the group to the kitchen. He counted heads. One person was missing. Father Thomas Pru. He dispatched Chevy Mato to summon the wayward priest. When the teenager didn't return, Foneman tramped off to find out what was causing the delay.

He received a partial answer as soon as he rounded the corner into the trucker hospitality area.

Down the hall, past the six sleeping rooms and the sole lavatory, the lower part of a pair of legs extended out of the doorway of the shower room. Foneman recognized Mato's faded blue jeans and sprinted to the restaurant employee's side.

The boy lay in the portion of the room used for dressing and undressing. He was breathing and did not have any visible signs of trauma. Foneman knelt beside him and called his name several times. Mato's eyes gradually opened and focused on the deputy.

"Are you alright?"

"Yeah," Mato said in a feeble voice before taking two deep breaths. "What happened?"

"I think you fainted. Seems to be a lot of that going around today. Stay down for a few minutes until your strength comes back. There's no need to get up now."

"Yes, there is. I gotta get up. I gotta get out of this place."

"Won't be long now before we'll all be out of here. The snow plows are on their way."

"No, no. This room. I gotta get out of this room." He tried to push himself up but didn't have the strength. "Help me get up. Please, please help me up."

"What's the big hurry?"

"Don't you see it?" Mato's eyes widened for a moment and then sunk shut.

"See what?"

No response.

Foneman, still kneeling at the teenager's side, scanned the vicinity for whatever was terrorizing Chevy Mato. At first he saw nothing. Then he focused on the closed plastic curtain separating the shower stall from the dressing area. Four human fingers protruded from underneath the curtain. Foneman stepped gingerly toward the stall. He pulled the curtain open just enough to look inside. No need to go any further. Father Thomas Pru was obviously dead.

The priest's body slumped against the wall in a sitting position, his eyes bulged, his tongue hung out of an open mouth. Pink gouges surrounded his neck, seemingly indicating an obvious cause of death. Strangulation. His belt had been removed and hung from an exposed three-inch pipe running across the ceiling, perhaps in a clumsy attempt to fake a suicide.

Foneman backed away a few steps, looked up at the bright light fixture, felt the room spin faster and faster, and keeled over backwards. His head banged off the wall before landing squarely on Mato's stomach.

* * * * *

Justin Foneman could not comprehend the embarrassment and downright humiliation awaiting him. He sat on the floor taking short sips from a straw with no concern for where the straw led or what the liquid was. His head ached. He sensed a lot of activity around him and could hear the clamor coming from several mouths at the same time. The words were too garbled to understand. He knew he wasn't home, but did not recognize his surroundings.

His recovery was slow. The first person he recognized was Margarita, then Tommy Glynn, and then Marky. Their blurred faces stared down at him. Several seconds elapsed before he realized he was a sheriff's deputy on duty. His first reaction was to feel for his gun. It was there, secure in the holster. His head rotated in slow motion toward the shower stall. The curtain was wide open. Who were all those people blocking his view? Glimpses of hands touching and pulling on a body. More hands removing the shower curtain from its rod. A dull flash. Suddenly it all came back.

"Stop it," he yelled with as much energy as he could muster, which was not enough to be heard over the mayhem.

"Stop it." Glynn's explosive voice evoked the desired response. All eyes turned toward him.

"Tell them to get out." Foneman sounded tired. "Tell them to get out."

Glynn did as ordered, adding a rough *And Now* at the end. Most of the offenders obeyed, sidestepping the deputy sitting on the floor as they left. One did not.

"Father Pru wants me to stay," Lannay Sargetti said. "He wants me to help get him to heaven."

"Get her out."

Glynn pulled Sargetti by the wrist. She did not physically resist, but voiced multiple arguments why she should be allowed to remain with the deceased priest. Glynn handed her over to Margarita and Ann Nussy with specific orders to usher her to the storeroom and not permit her to leave. He returned to the shower room after making a brief detour to the kitchen to retrieve two chairs.

"Boy, I really screwed up."

Glynn could hear the fatigue and despair in the deputy's voice. "No you didn't. In order to screw up you have to be aware of what you are doing and do it willingly. Did you will yourself to pass out?"

"Of course not."

"And you were unconscious, weren't you?"

"I like your way of thinking." Foneman tried to force a smile.

He allowed Glynn to help him to his feet and surveyed the immediate vicinity. Pru's body was no longer leaning against the wall. He assumed the priest's remains were under the lumpy shower curtain near his feet. "Who moved him?"

"The truck drivers and the ghost chaser. Something about making it easier for his spirit to get out of his body."

"And they put the curtain on him?"

"Sharon Minder did. Just now. She was also trying to close his eyes."

"Fantastic. They completely contaminated the crime scene while I slept on the floor." His words were labored and fatigued.

"Let's sit down for a few minutes. You look like you're about ready to pass out again." Glynn guided the shaky man to the chairs he had placed in the hallway.

"I must have bonked my head pretty hard." He gently tapped a tender spot on the back of his head. "Ouch."

They sat in silence, Foneman taking an occasional deep breath. The manager of the Midway Truck and Traveler Oasis was at a loss for words. The law officer was still fighting to regain his full strength and mental capacity.

Foneman spoke first. "Where did everybody go?"

"I herded the whole bunch into the storeroom and shut the door. Probably should have locked them in."

"Not such a bad idea. We have to keep them from coming back here and doing more damage."

"Should I really lock them in?"

"As tempting as it is, we better not. Might be construed as false imprisonment or unlawful detainment. That phone of yours doesn't work back here, does it?"

"No, you have to be in the kitchen."

"Hate to do it, but I suppose I better get my butt in there and call the office. Give them the bad news."

"Don't have to. They already know. Mrs. Minder called them. Twice. Once to tell them what happened. The second time to tell them you were awake."

"Wonderful, absolutely wonderful." Foneman slumped in his chair. "I'll be the laughing stock of the entire sheriff's department, and probably every cop in the United States."

"They'll understand."

"Maybe to my face. Behind my back is a different story."

"What if you were to catch the killer?"

"Fat chance of that happening."

Tommy Glynn accompanied the slow-walking Justin Foneman on an inspection tour of the barricaded doors. The one leading to the repair garage was undisturbed. No one had entered or left that way. The same was true of the one at the opposite end of the hallway leading to the parking lot. And the tables stacked against the swinging doors in the kitchen remained in place.

"That leaves the overhead door in the storeroom," Foneman said. "You know what it means if the stuff stacked against that door hasn't been moved?"

"I do. It means someone in this restaurant is the murderer."

"Quite possibly a serial killer."

*****

Glynn and Foneman encountered the exact opposite of what they had been expecting when they opened the storeroom door. Cold silence. Concerned but not panicked faces. A few standees in the back due to the shortage of chairs. Josh Byner playing on the floor with empty Styrofoam cups.

Both men shifted their sight toward the barricade against the overhead door. Glynn thought it looked untouched. Foneman noticed a few cartons at the far end were askew, not sufficient enough to indicate that someone had tried to leave, but just enough to have been nudged out of place by Dontae Dakota and the youngest Nussy during their earlier tête-à-tête at that precise spot. Foneman had hoped he would find clear evidence that someone had escaped through the loading dock door. He counted heads. Fifteen. The killer was still in the building, and, more than likely, sitting or standing in front of him.

Foneman drafted a crew to haul the chairs and small restaurant tables to the storeroom from their temporary location in the kitchen. The room was cramped, but now contained enough tables and seats for everyone. Larry Nussy ignored the vacant chair and continued to pace in the meager open space at the back of the room. The deputy asked him to join the others at the tables.

Foneman looked at his watch. Twenty minutes past five. Without making any comments about Father Pru's death or his own spell of unconsciousness, he told them to tear out a piece of paper from the notebook Tommy Glynn was passing around. They were to write on the paper when and under what circumstances was the last time they saw Tom Pru and, in very specific details, what they saw, did, touched and took from the room where his body was found. Glynn supplied pens to those who needed one. Fifteen minutes later he collected the pages.

Next came Foneman's brief speech. A large cadre of law enforcement officers was en route and should arrive in the not too distant future. Everyone was confined to the storeroom until the reinforcements took possession of the building. In about an hour Tommy Glynn would bring in snacks and sandwich fixings. If someone absolutely had to use the restroom, he would personally accompany that person to the lavatory. He concluded his lecture by convincingly stating that anyone leaving the storeroom without his explicit permission was subject to being shot, no exceptions. He ended abruptly, without asking for comments or questions.

The detainees observed Foneman silently reading their reports as though they were a frightened class of third graders watching a persnickety teacher scrutinize their grammar tests. The responses to his first question were surprisingly consistent. The last Father Pru was seen alive was about twenty minutes before his body was discovered. At that time he was sitting alone at the same table where the deputy had observed him writing in his Bible. Only one oddity had occurred. Before the priest disappeared, he had lent his Bible to Sharon Minder.

The second question helped Foneman establish what had occurred while he lay unconscious on the floor. Chevy Mato did not return to the shower room after he regained his strength and alerted everyone to what he had thought was a double death. He had mistakenly informed them that, in addition to the priest, the deputy had also expired. Marky, Dakota, and Sargetti admitted they had readjusted Pru's corpse. Sharon Minder confirmed she had covered Pru with the shower curtain after trying to shut his eyes. Several others confessed to attempting to take his pulse or touching his skin to see if he was cold. Only the three Nussys mentioned the strangulation marks. Nothing was reported to have been removed.

Foneman asked Sharon Minder to step into the hallway for a private conversation. "You wrote that Father Pru gave you his Bible the last time you saw him."

"I asked if I could borrow it."

"Why?"

"Reading scriptures helps me calm down. It almost always works. My Bible is in the glove compartment of our car."

"Where was he when he gave it to you?"

"Almost exactly where we are standing now. I just left a sleeping room. He was headed in the direction of the lavatory. He asked if I had a good sleep and I said no. That's when I told him I read scripture when I'm nervous and asked if I could use his Bible."

"Did he say anything when he handed it to you?"

"Only that I was welcome to use it while he took care of other business."

"Nothing else?"

"The Old Testament was good for soothing nerves, the New Testament for seeking answers. He said the Bible had an answer for every question, but you must look in the right place to find it. Then he walked away."

"To the lavatory?"

"I assume so, but I wasn't watching him."

"Where's the Bible now?"

"I'm not sure. I had it with me when we all ran into the shower to see what happened. I must have left it there."

"So it's still in the shower room?"

"My husband thought he saw that spooky woman pick it up, but he might be wrong. She doesn't have it now."

Foneman cornered Lannay Sargetti and confronted her about the missing Bible. She said she had seen Sharon Minder take the book into the shower room and found it on the floor next to Pru's body after Minder left. She gave it to Dontae Dakota, who put in the kitchen where Sharon had been sitting instead of giving it directly to her.

The deputy picked up the sheet of paper on which Sargetti had written the responses to his two questions. "You failed to mention you removed the Bible from the shower room," he said.

"I thought you were asking about things that were there before Father Pru's death. Sharon Minder brought it in after he died. I was merely returning a misplaced item."

Foneman accepted the explanation and allowed Sargetti to return to the storeroom. He found the book in plain view on a food preparation counter in the kitchen and flipped through the pages before shaking it vigorously to dislodge any loose items. A novena prayer card and a bookmark depicting Saint Michael the Archangel dropped out. The Bible had to be preserved as possible evidence. Finding no other secure place in the kitchen, he unlocked the pantry and placed the book on the bottom shelf of the table holding Jon Silton's remains.

The phone in the kitchen rang as he was returning to the storeroom. He hesitated to answer it. A sinking feeling overwhelmed him. He was sure it was Detective Lorenz. He braced himself to face the music, which might turn out to be a funeral dirge for his law enforcement career

* * * * *

The music was much sweeter than Justin Foneman had imagined. Karen Lorenz was unexpectedly sympathetic to his predicament. She complimented his decision to confine the group to one place, overcrowded and uncomfortable as it was. She also applauded him for making them record their recollections while they were still fresh and untainted by the opinions and experiences of others.

Lorenz was curious about Lannay Sargetti's written summary. Foneman read it to her word by word. The ghost chaser had admitted enticing the two semi drivers to change the position of Pru's body, an action that could or could not be considered incriminating, depending on her motive. Lorenz was more concerned about her written and oral ramblings then about her contacts with the spiritual world.

"I'm not qualified to judge her level of sanity," the detective said, "but Sargetti may be crazy enough to wreak some havoc. She told you she wanted to be at someone's side when they died. Perhaps she arranged to do so."

"Maybe crazy enough," Foneman said, "but not strong enough to do it herself. Wait until you see her. She'd have trouble lifting a ten pound sack of potatoes."

Lorenz also asked to have Allie and Jager Rellik's reports read to her. The phrasing of their responses was different but the content was identical. Neither could remember when they had seen Pru last. Both followed the rest of the mob to the shower room after Chevy Mato emotionally pronounced the priest and the deputy had died. They entered the room only far enough to catch brief glimpses of Foneman and Pru, after which they retreated to their usual table in the kitchen.

"Did you confirm their story?"

"I haven't confirmed anyone's story. I've been too busy keeping them alive and away from the body."

"Where were the Relliks about the time Pru was murdered?"

"I suppose they were at that same little restaurant table that was moved into the kitchen. They've always been there. I haven't seen them any place else."

"What about when Silton was killed? Any idea what they were doing then?"

"I didn't ask. How could I? No one knows when, or for that matter where, Silton died."

"Except the murderer or murderers."

"True, but why the sudden interest in Allie and Jager Rellik? They seem a little off-the-wall like a lot of other young people nowadays, but a double homicide? They're not on the top of my list of suspects."

"You're probably correct. It could be a mere coincidence."

"What could be a coincidence?"

"Call me a nerd, but I like to play with words and letters. I do crossword puzzles, letter scrambles, and play Scrabble and other such games. Simply by accident I noticed something really odd about the Rellik name." She went no further.

"So, are you going to tell me?"

"Look at it for a few seconds."

He spent more than a few seconds studying the name. "I give up. I'm not seeing anything."

"What is Rellik spelled backwards?"

"K-I-L . . ." Foneman stopped abruptly. "Well, I'll be damned. K-I-L-L-E-R. Killer."

* * * * *

Detective Lorenz's advice delighted Justin Foneman. Do nothing about the fascinating discovery about the Rellik name. In fact, do nothing about pursuing any suspects. She will do that when she arrives, which she thought would be

145

in less than two hours. Foneman's sole goal should be keeping the people at the truck stop in place and safe. None of them should be permitted to leave, even if it became possible to do so.

The conversation with Lorenz eased the Deputy's anxiety. With his notepad in hand, he entered the storeroom confident he could maintain control of those in his care for the next couple of hours. No further harm would come to any of them. He did not foresee the group's emotional rollercoaster was about to take another precipitous dive.

"Finally!" Ann Nussy shot up from her chair. "Have you found the killer?"

"No, I've been . . ."

Kelly Nussy didn't allow Foneman to finish. "Why not? Are you waiting for another one of us to be murdered?"

"I think . . . "

"What about her?" Ann swung an accusing finger in Sharon Minder's direction. "Why did you pull her out of the room? I saw her carrying the priest's Bible. Did she have something to do with all of this?"

Jim Minder clinched and slightly raised his fists as he started toward Ann Nussy. "My wife had nothing to do with anything. She has never hurt a soul."

Dontae Dakota reacted quickly to block his path.

Minder stopped short of making contact with the beefy truck driver. "If I were you," he said to

Ann while glaring over Dakota's shoulder, "I would take a closer look at my own family before I start I accusing anyone else."

Turmoil erupted. Loud voices came from all directions. More people rose from their chairs. Justin Foneman held his hands high in an effort to silence the mob, but it was Marky's piercing whistle that quieted the crowd.

"We may be getting bent out of shape for no reason," Marky said. "We don't know if these men have been murdered. You all saw the belt hanging from the pipe. Maybe the priest hung himself. And the shot that killed the other guy could have been self-inflicted."

"Priests don't kill themselves," Jim Minder said. "Suicide is a mortal sin, and priests aren't supposed to commit mortal sins."

"I think they changed that," his wife Sharon said. "Suicide is no longer a mortal sin."

"Where have you been for the last few years?" Jade Byner said. "Clergy sexual abuse is rampant. Priests aren't always as holy as they are made out to be."

"They are only human like the rest of us," Margarita said.

"Pru didn't hang himself." All eyes turned toward Kelly Nussy after her loud assertion. She was about to pour gasoline on the smoldering fire. "I saw the marks on his neck. They were made by something like a rope, not the wide belt on the pipe. Besides, the belt was hanging straight down, not in a noose."

"I told you," her mother said. "It *was* murder."

"If it was murder," Larry Nussy added, "that makes one of us the killer, right?"

Heads twisted in every direction, searching for the person most likely to commit such a heinous crime as murdering a man of the cloth.

"Now wait a minute," the deputy said. "You're all jumping to conclusions. We have not determined the cause of death for either man. For all we know, they could have died accidentally, so don't get yourself worked up for nothing."

Ann Nussy went on the attack. "Accidentally? Maybe the first guy, but the priest? No way. He was murdered." Five or six other people chimed in their agreement. "And, as my husband said, that means one of us is a murderer."

Foneman recognized he was up against a brick wall. "Let's suppose you're right. Suppose it was murder. That doesn't mean the killer has to be in this room."

Ann would not relinquish her stranglehold on the deputy. "Oh yeah. Where would he be?"

"Lots of places to hide around here. The repair garage. The store. Maybe outside in a car."

"And how did he get out of this little fort of ours with all these boxes and other junk blocking his way? We didn't see or hear anyone coming or going."

"Not necessarily."

"Baloney."

Foneman ignored the degrading comment. "Remember there's safety in numbers. If we stick together, no one will get hurt." In his peripheral vision he saw Ann Nussy edging toward the doorway. "Only a fool will try to pull something in plain view of so many witnesses."

The timing could not have been more perfect. The storeroom went completely dark. Assorted screams and cuss words ricocheted from corner to corner until the lights went back on a few seconds later.

Ann Nussy's hand rested on the light switch. "Look how easy it is. We've all seen it on TV. A bunch of people together in a room. The lights go out, followed by a gunshot or a loud scream. Lights come back on. Someone is dead. That's exactly what happened in that play I was telling you about."

"And in that midnight movie that was on TV last Saturday night," Chevy Mato said, "the one about the high school kids in Mexico."

Ann's action was enough to push Foneman over the edge. "That's enough," he pronounced with authority. "We are not talking about imaginary tales here. This is real life, and those things don't happen in real life." He glared at the offending woman. "Don't ever turn those lights off again."

"No need to blow a gasket."

"I side with the lawman," Marky said. "You're all forgetting one key thing. I was outside when I was shot. All of you were inside. The shooter can't be in this room."

"Maybe there are two of them," Ann said. "One outside and one inside."

Foneman blew up. "Sit down and shut up! Everybody sit down and shut up."

One person did not obey. Lannay Sargetti crept up to the deputy. "Give me ten minutes alone with Father Pru. He'll tell me what happened."

"Sit down!"

* * * * *

Something about the latest insurrection troubled Justin Foneman. At first he thought it was Ann Nussy's prank with the lights. It reminded him of Karen Lorenz's report about the power outages the blizzard had caused in other parts of the county. A blackout would give the murderer an opportunity to kill again. That fact alone was disconcerting, but he was made even more apprehensive by the realization that the target of the assassin could very well be the only living law enforcement person on site. Him.

Despite his trepidation about a blackout, Foneman was convinced something more sinister than an improbable power failure was bothering him. He could not put his finger on it. Something had happened during the outburst that would enable a good detective to pounce on the perpetrator and make an arrest. But he was not a good detective. He was not any kind of a detective. How could he be expected to notice the perpetrator's tiny slipup? On the other hand, he had an overwhelming notion he was on the verge of breaking the case wide open.

Foneman replayed the brief episode over and over in his mind, trying to recall the precise words and actions of each of the characters. He concentrated on his top seven suspects, namely Jade Byner, Dontae Dakota, Lannay Sargetti, Ann Nussy, Kelly Nussy, and most recently, the two Relliks. Their individual behaviors ranged from obnoxious to reserved, but nothing they had said or done made them stand out as the guilty party.

"Hurry, mommy." Little Josh pulled on Jade's sleeve. "I have to go potty."

"Take him," Foneman said. "We can't let the little man wet his pants. Come right back. I'll watch you from here." Foneman sat alone at the two-person table he had pulled over to the storeroom's doorway to impede any attempted departure and to give him a clear line of sight down the hallway all the way to the repair shop.

Kelly Nussy raised her hand. "What about me?"

"What about you?"

"The kid's not the only one who needs to use the bathroom."

"Well, I need to treat everybody the same, so I guess I have to watch you go potty, too."

The remark was greeted with chuckles. Kelly blushed. "I don't have to go any more, pervert."

"Oh no, it's too late," Dontae Dakota said. "Somebody get a sponge and a bucket." More laughter.

Kelly's pink face darkened to bright red. Her middle finger shot high in the air.

"Settle down folks," Foneman said. The humorous exchange served to relieve some of the tension in the air, but he did not want to lose control of the group again. He waited for mother and son to return before he began to review his notes from the one-on-one interviews he had been conducting when someone took a shot at Marky. Three readings of the notes produced no new leads or theories.

The deputy glanced up from his work to see fourteen adults starring at him in utter silence. The scene reminded him of the handful of times he had been sentenced to detention hall in high school, usually for exacting his own form of discipline on misbehaving peers. The students in detention had nothing to do but look at the teacher, who of course was the most feared and callous adult in the entire school.

"When I told you to be quiet, you know, I didn't mean you couldn't chat or play games with each other. You need to be civil and respectful, that's all." No one stirred.

"Go ahead, I won't hurt you, as long as you follow the rules." He sounded like a detention hall teacher. "Go on."

A few whispered conversations began. They gradually became louder. Dontae Dakota walked over to get the checkerboard. Kelly Nussy put in her ear buds. No one dared mention the murders. Foneman went back to his papers.

This time he was reading the narratives each person had written about his or her contact with

Father Pru. Nothing close to a smoking gun. He thought about his own last contact with the priest. Pru appeared to be quite peaceful as he wrote in the margins of his Bible, unaware of the evil about to befall him. Once again, nothing.

Foneman sighed in frustration. The answer was there, staring him in the face. He was absolutely certain of that. He was so close, but, as his wise grandfather used to say, close only counts in horseshoes.

* * * * *

"Deputy," Ann Nussy said, "it's been over an hour. Whatever happened to that food you said we were going to get?"

"Did I say that? What do you think, Mr. Glynn? Do you have any grub you can give these starving people?"

"I'm sure I will be able to put together something, as long as I can have my two capable assistants helping me."

"Go. Take Margarita and Chevy with you."

The waitress slipped Foneman a note written on a page torn from her food order pad as she passed his table. *Don't forget that Jade girl. I told you she was playing peek-a-boo with that first man before he died. I also heard her and the priest laughing behind the closed door of the room she was supposed to be sleeping in. Then he died. She's up to no good if you ask me.*

The message hit Foneman like a knockout punch. Why wasn't he looking harder for a link between the two victims?

Margarita was right. Jade Byner had a connection with each of the deceased men. Jon Silton was from her hometown and had been hired by her father to follow her. She might have recognized him in the restaurant. Later she and the priest were doing something together in a locked room. Pru said she was confessing her sins, but Margarita heard them laughing. Both men are dead. What a coincidence. Assuming the waitress was telling the truth.

Foneman concocted a possible progression of events. Byner confronts Silton. They argue. He threatens to call her father. She shoots him in the back and pretends to find him in the parking lot. She confesses the crime to Father Pru. He threatens to turn her in. She strangles him. Or maybe, instead of confessing, she and Pru are getting to know each other, biblically speaking, in the courtesy sleeping room. Or maybe it's not consensual. Could he be using what he learned during confession to blackmail her for sex? Either way, she ends up killing him.

More Jade Byner scenarios surfaced like bubbles rising in boiling water. What if she murdered Tom Pru in a fit of rage because he was the father of her child? Or what if the story about her male cohort being a Canadian was only a ruse to cover up an illicit relationship with a married man in her own hometown? Jon Silton, for example. Too far fetched, Foneman decided.

Who else had ties to both victims? Earlier he thought Kelly Nussy might have a romantic attraction to Pru, but even if she did, he was aware of no link to Silton. The priest spent a great deal of time trying to convert Marky. Was that sufficient reason for a strangling? If so, how was he connected to the dead cop? And how did he end up getting shot? The priest's approach may have irritated a few individuals from time to time, but overall he was friendly with everyone at the truck stop, and that made it difficult to pin down a suspect for his murder.

"Watch out," a male voice shouted from the kitchen. The scream of a woman in trouble instantly followed.

Foneman knocked over his table as he sprang to his feet. "Everyone stay here," he yelled as he slammed the door to the storeroom. He advanced into the kitchen in a crouch, his gun drawn. Chevy Mato and Tommy Glynn were glaring down at the floor, presumably at Margarita, since she was the only other person who was given permission to be in the room. Foneman assumed the worst.

"Hands in the air."

"It was an accident," Mato said.

"I said hands up."

The pair chose to comply rather than try to explain.

"I'm mostly okay." Margarita was talking and giggling at the same time.

"What's going on?"

"She dropped a bowl full of mustard on the floor and slipped in it," Glynn said. "It really was an accident."

The fallen waitress continued to snicker. A puddle of yellow mustard surrounded the broken bowl. A glob of it glazed the sole of her left shoe. Pieces of sliced ham and turkey decorated the floor around her. A tray of cheese was still intact.

"You can put your hands down."

Glynn and Foneman expressed concern for the waitress's well being while helping her up. She countered with self-deprecating remarks about her own clumsiness. Without being told, Chevy Mato began cleaning the mess. A thin piece of ham clinging to Margarita's backside caused him to howl with contagious laughter. Soon all four convulsed in amusement.

After the merriment subsided, Foneman filled pitchers with soda pop and water while the three restaurant employees replenished the meat platter with fresh ham and turkey. Together they loaded an aluminum cart with sandwich fixings, potato chips, beverage pitchers, and the cupcakes intended for the ill-fated earlier celebration.

"Who's there?" Larry Nussy shouted when the storeroom door opened. He and the other terrified strandees were hiding behind a wall of tables tipped on their sides.

"It's me," Foneman said. "And the food."

Dontae Dakota's head popped above the temporary wall. "It's him alright. And the people who work here. They have chow."

"What happened out there?" Nussy asked from behind the table.

"False alarm." Foneman described the incident, saying that Glynn had shouted the warning when he saw the waitress was about to step on the slippery mustard and Margarita had screamed as she fell.

One by one the others emerged from their hiding places, still wary about their own safety. A few made comments about how the deputy's abrupt actions had frightened them. After righting the tables, they waited patiently for the Oasis staff to wheel in the food.

Once everyone seemed settled, Foneman asked Marky and Tommy Glynn to guard the doorway while he returned to the kitchen to make a few phone calls. He instructed them not to let anyone out of the storeroom. If a visit to the lavatory was absolutely necessary, and he stressed the word *absolutely*, one of them should accompany the distressed person to and from the restroom.

* * * * *

The first call was to Stefanie. Foneman knew the sheriff's office had notified his wife a few hours earlier that he would be working a double shift. Now he informed her that, due to the horrendous weather conditions, it would probably expand to a triple or quadruple shift. When she asked what he was doing, he only told her he was guarding a crime scene until the big brass could get there. He was relieved Stefanie did not request more details. The less she knew, the better. He was scared enough for the two of them. No need to alarm her.

The second call went to the home of Detective Karen Lorenz. Her husband answered the phone. "We made it to the county road on snowshoes, and the snowplow picked her up maybe fifteen minutes ago. The driver was not a happy camper. He claimed the conditions were the worst he's ever seen. He used the term *vile*."

"I thought it stopped snowing."

"It did, but the wind hasn't diminished much. It's still blowing like a hurricane and whipping around snow that fell hours ago. Visibility is better than when it was snowing, but it's still difficult to see. The plow driver thought the roads would be plugged again within forty-five minutes of opening them."

"Shoot."

"Plus the windchill is making it feel colder than an artic glacier. I flipped on the TV news as soon as I got back home, just in time to hear Awesome Austin report windchills in the twenty-five to thirty-five below range throughout the area."

"Wonderful."

"All I can tell you for sure is they're going to try their darnedest to get to you. I'm hoping they can, but Mother Nature may have other ideas."

Foneman closed the conversation with some unkind words about Mother Nature. The last call went to the sheriff's office.

"With the exception of your site," Kadence the dispatcher said, "the entire county is exceptionally quiet. Of course, a few small patches don't have phone service or electricity, but everyone seems to be hunkering down to wait out the storm. Which is good, because we can't get to them anyway."

"Haven't tried my radio lately. Is that any better?"

"Somewhat, but still a lot of static. Same with cell phones. Your best bet is the landline, although they are also chancy. The circuits were overloaded earlier when everyone in the county was trying to talk at the same time, but they've been pretty much open all afternoon. Come to think of it, they could have been out and I didn't know it. Do you want to hear some good news?"

"Good news? You're kidding?"

"Reinforcements are here. Sergeant Wyatt had quite an ordeal but finally made it into the office. So did the rookie whose patrol car was stuck in a snowdrift up north. Both said the driving was treacherous, akin to driving on a sudsy washboard at five miles per hour."

Kadence transferred Foneman to the newly arrived duty sergeant. Wyatt was in the underground garage shifting crime scene gear from the department's van to an SUV. He was concerned about the van's stability and traction on the slippery roads. The plan was for Wyatt and the rookie deputy to follow the state snowplow carrying Detective Lorenz to the truck stop. They weren't going to wait for the trooper who was still too far away. The state plow had already arrived, so they would leave immediately once Karen Lorenz showed up.

The sergeant reinforced what Lorenz's husband had told Foneman. Visibility was poor, travel conditions miserable. Highway 94 would not be open for normal usage until several hours after the wind died down. The drivers of the two plows, one from the north and one from the south, were instructed not to dally at the truck stop. They needed to prepare for the big push to get the roads cleared once the storm ends. The law officers they were escorting to the Truck and Traveler Oasis would be marooned there for quite some time.

Wyatt had no new suggestions for what Foneman could do to keep the folks at the Oasis compliant and safe. "In your case," he said, "the blizzard is your best friend and your worst enemy. It makes it easy for you to retain all witnesses and suspects on site, but it also means the murdering bastard is somewhere very close to you."

* * * * *

Kelly Nussy assailed Justin Foneman on his return to the storeroom. "Did I hear you say you were making phone calls?"

"What business is that of yours?"

"I want to call a close friend."

"Use your cell phone."

"I have tried. Thousands of times. It hasn't worked since we got here."

Her mother Ann joined the fray. "I thought the lines were dead."

"They were, but they're back up now, at least for the time being. It's one of those on-again-off-again things."

"So, as long as they're up, let my daughter call her friend. What harm will that do?"

"If I let one person use the phone, I'll have to let everyone use it. I can't do that. The line has to be kept open for police business."

His own words made the deputy realize he might not hear the phone ring from where he was sitting in the storeroom.

"How many of you want to make a phone call?" Ann asked.

Foneman sensed another insurrection was about to occur, but only Kelly, Marky, Jade Byner and Lannay Sargetti raised their hands.

Ann Nussy was also surprised. "You can't let four people make a short phone call?" Her sarcasm was unmistakable.

"Let me think about it."

A few minutes later Foneman consented to the proposition if the four agreed to certain stipulations. His table would be moved down the hallway to the backdoor of the kitchen. The caller would sit at a table inside the kitchen but as close to the hall as the phone reception would allow. He would watch and listen to the caller. The conversation would last no more than three minutes. No mention could be made of the two dead bodies.

"Doing it your way doesn't give us much privacy," Kelly said.

"That's not correct," Foneman responded. "Doing it my way gives you no privacy whatsoever. It's your choice. Do you want privacy or do you want to talk to your boyfriend?"

"How did you know it was a guy?"

Foneman shrugged. "Fifty-fifty chance."

Kelly smacked her lips. "Oh, alright. Can I go first?"

"You may. But if you overstep the boundaries you ruin it for yourself and everyone else."

She dramatically sauntered to the appointed table, punched in a series of numbers, and feigned impatience as she waited for her friend to answer. Twirling her hair with her index finger, she proceeded to tell the other person how much she missed him and couldn't wait to get back in his arms. She used thinly veiled sexual innuendos to describe what the two would do when reunited. Her wide eyes focused on Foneman for the entire three minutes, causing him to wonder if the language was primarily intended to shock him or tease the boy on the phone. He also didn't know if she was speaking to her ex-fiancé or a new gent she had already lined up to replace him.

"Got to say goodbye now. The dumb cop who's listening to me is either giving me the signal to hang up or he is trying to slash his throat with his own finger." Kelly thumped the phone on the table.

Foneman had made no such slashing motion. He shot to his feet, face livid, and pointed an accusing finger at the woman. "Why did you say that?"

"Don't know." She wriggled her shoulders and brushed against the deputy as she rejoined her parents in the storeroom.

"Watch it, missy. You're pushing the envelope."

Foneman braced himself for a sharp rebuttal from Kelly's mother, but Ann Nussy must have decided it was in her best interest as well as her daughter's not to challenge the infuriated officer.

The other three phone calls were made without incident. Marky called his wife and promised he would not leave the Oasis until it was absolutely safe to drive his giant rig. He sounded excited about his new idea for his next mystery novel that would be so real it would "scare the pants off" his readers. Foneman could tell Marky was itching to tell his spouse about the murders.

Jade Byner obtained permission from Foneman to allow Josh to say hello to her parents. She must have coached her son to say he was at home. Jade did the same, making reference to being at her apartment in Minneapolis. Apparently, her parents chose not to call her bluff or were unaware Silton had trailed her to the truck stop.

Lannay's call must have been to the ghost chaser she was on her way to visit. She hoped they would see a real ghost when they finally met in Sauk Centre. She gushed about feeling the presence of spirits during her trip, but did not spill the beans about the dead men at the truck stop.

To Foneman's astonishment, no one else made a last minute appeal to use the phone.

* * * * *

Although he considered moving his small table back to the doorway of the storeroom, a distance of only twenty feet, Foneman opted to keep it in the hallway near the kitchen. He needed to hear the phone ring when Detective Lorenz called.

The opportunity he afforded the strandees to make phone calls combined with the sandwiches and cupcakes eased, but did not come close to eradicating, the tension at the truck stop. How could the deputy expect any better? Two people dead. Their killer or killers nearby faking innocence. He reaffirmed his decision to let Karen Lorenz and the other detectives do the investigating. He would simply keep the peace until they arrived. However, despite his efforts to ignore it, Tommy Glynn's earlier assertion relentlessly assailed his mind. Redemption could be gained by catching the killer. He rocked back and forth as he sat alone in the hallway, once again weighing his options. What harm could come from taking one last stab at it?

Marky was seated at the front table in the storeroom making a third attempt at writing an outline for his new novel. He looked up when the approaching deputy stopped to lean against the adjacent wall. "Want me to relieve you for a while?"

"No, you look busy."

"I can write out there as easily as I can in here, maybe even better. Fewer distractions."

"Sounds like one of those win-win deals you were talking about earlier. I'd appreciate the break.

My back's a little stiff. Come get me if the phone in the kitchen rings."

Foneman squeezed around the tables squashed together in the storeroom. He first paused to chat with the Relliks and successfully avoided the temptation to reveal the secret he knew about their name. As usual, they were uncommunicative, so he quickly moved on. Ann and Kelly Nussy were overly lavish in expressing their gratitude for allowing the younger of the two to phone her friend. Perhaps they were trying to make amends for their past behavior.

Lannay Sargetti begged Foneman to permit her to spend some time with the dead priest. She struggled to convince him the deceased man's spirit would disappear forever as soon as the other law enforcement personnel began poking around his body. Foneman made the mistake of challenging Sargetti. If spirits disappear shortly after people pass away, how can she expect to see the ghosts of those who died many years ago at the haunted sites she was planning on visiting? He instantly regretted the decision and needed all his ingenuity to extract himself from her longwinded and convoluted explanation.

Chevy Mato offered Foneman the last cupcake, but the deputy, thinking of all the sweets he had already consumed at the Oasis, declined.

"Have you made plans for what you are going to do after high school?"

"Not yet," Mato said. "I'm only a sophomore." A slight smile crossed his face. "Although after today I know two jobs I will never consider." He waited for the deputy to respond.

"Okay, what are they?"

"Cop and doctor. I hate being around dying and dead people, and I don't want to be killed by some homicidal nut."

"Can't argue about that. I feel the same way"

Foneman looked across the table at Sharon Minder. "How you doing?"

"Get me the hell out of here," she said.

"And not in a body bag," added her husband Jim.

"I'm doing my best, ma'am." Foneman skirted his way back to the hall and pulled up a chair across from Marky.

"Back so soon?"

"Yeah, the natives are restless. Guess I can't blame them. How are you holding up?"

"As good as I can with a sore arm and two dead men in the building. Writing about murders is a lot less nerve racking than being around them."

"You're not giving up on your dream, are you?"

"No way, dude. Look at this." He held up several loose pages covered with handwriting. "I've got lots of good stuff. And it's all real. All I have to do is make a story out of it. No more rejection letters for this fellow."

"Still planning on writing about our adventure?"

"Why not?" It's a perfect setting. A lonely truck stop. A blizzard. No one can get in or out. People start dropping dead. Everyone's a suspect. Can't help but be a best seller."

"The bad guy still a truck driver?"

"I'm waiting for things to play out here first. You know, see who killed the two men and why. I may invent a completely different ending if it's not exciting enough."

"What if we never find out?"

"I'll say the deputy sheriff did it." Both men chuckled. "It worked in that play the old lady Nussy was talking about. The cop was the killer."

"What if these guys weren't murdered?"

"Pretty obvious the priest was strangled, wasn't it?"

"Seems that way, but quite often things aren't what they seem. Are you going to strangle a priest in your book?"

"Absolutely. Makes a good story. I'll probably change the first one, though. Replace the cop with a terrorist on his way to plant a bomb some place, but still let him get shot in the neck like the cop was. That's a better storyline. A priest and a terrorist. It has to be a best seller."

"As long as you're changing things, make the deputy a handsome, young guy with lots of brains. Make sure he solves the case. And maybe saves a gorgeous woman or two during the process. You have my permission to use my name to make it realistic."

"You should write your own book. Then you can paint the deputy anyway you want."

"I could make myself a superhero."

"I bet you'd be a good mystery writer with all the experience you have sheriffing." Marky saw Dontae Dakota waving a checkerboard in his direction. "Think about it," he said as he left to accept Dakota's challenge. "You could make a million dollars."

Foneman checked his watch. If all goes right, Lorenz and company should be arriving soon, no more than sixty minutes he hoped. He was exhausted, physically and mentally. The pendulum swung again. He was back to not wanting to think about the murders any more. He only cared about going home to Stefanie.

After a while he began to muse about Marky's suggestion. Maybe, when he retired, he would write a book. Many years ago he really enjoyed being a reporter on his high school newspaper, and his teachers had always praised his writing skills and creativity.

Marky, of course, was wrong about his experience with the sheriff's department. Almost all his work was so mundane. The occasional drunk driver or theft from a lake cabin was not exciting enough fodder for a mystery story. Neither was the runaway bull he had to corral one rainy April afternoon or the traffic jams he needed to unsnarl after every Independence Day fireworks display. The only major crime he ever encountered was the one in which he was currently mired.

The more he reflected on the idea, the more he liked it. He could author his own version of the murders at the Midway Truck and Traveler Oasis.

He would modify the details enough so they would not be a factual accounting of the crimes. As Marky had suggested, he might be better off changing the occupations of the victims. Make them more sinister.

"Holy shit," Foneman said loud enough to raise a few eyebrows in the storeroom. His next thought was kept completely to himself. *I know who the killer is.*

* * * * *

His arms extended in an imaginary stretch. In reality, Justin Foneman was scrutinizing the room, making a mental note of where every person was sitting and what they were doing. Half empty food trays and beverage pitchers rested on the few cardboard cartons that were not part of the massive barricade blocking the overhead door to the loading dock. Used paper plates and plastic utensils were stuffed into a nearby trash bag.

Trying to appear nonchalant, Foneman wedged his way toward Jim Minder and Tommy Glynn, who were deep in a conversation about the merits of spending their retirements in sunny Arizona.

"Sorry to interrupt you," he said. "I would like to borrow Mr. Glynn for a few minutes if you don't mind."

"How can I help you, deputy?" Glynn said.

"I need to show you something." He led the Oasis manager to the overhead door while paying attention to who was and was not watching them. "The soft drink pitchers are almost empty."

"I'll have Chevy take care of them right away."

"No, I would like you to fill them. I will help you."

Glynn recognized the request was a ploy to isolate him from the crowd. Plastic pitchers in hand, they passed into the kitchen, leaving the table in the hallway unmanned. Neither spoke until they reached the soda dispenser.

"More pop is not the reason we are here, is it?" Glynn's shaky voice was caused by a mixture of concern and curiosity.

"I'd like to ask you a few things. In confidence, of course. You must not tell another soul what we are going to talk about, unless I give you permission or a court orders you to do so, both of which I hope happen sooner than later."

Glynn did not respond or look at the deputy. He appeared to be concentrating on replenishing one of the pitchers with sugar free cola. He actually was calculating the risks and repercussions of the request. Something big was about to happen, and he did not want to put himself in any danger. The thought of receiving a court order alarmed him.

Foneman could wait no longer. "Well?"

"Well what?" Tommy Glynn was buying time. He was afraid of the unknown. Every extra second was needed to rally enough courage to tell the deputy he would not cooperate. He had to think of himself and his family.

"Do you agree to keep my questions confidential or not?"

Glynn ground his teeth while staring at the floor. "Okay. I reluctantly agree." He decided he had to at least appear to be accommodating.

"All I ask is that you tell the truth."

"And keep it quiet."

"At least for the immediate future. Tell nobody about our conversation. I don't want my suspect to get away before I can build my case against him."

"Okay. I understand." Glynn was unnerved by the deputy's words. His face tightened.

"Were you in the food pantry this morning when I found a wound on the back of the first dead man?"

"Yes, you know I was."

"Who else was there when I found the wound?"

"No one. Only you and me."

"Do you remember what I said about the wound?"

"First you said the man might have fallen on something sharp. Then you said it looked like he had been shot."

"Who did you tell about my gunshot theory?"

"I don't recall telling anyone. No, I'm positive I didn't tell anyone. You asked me to keep it quiet."

"Only you and I know he may have been shot in the neck?"

"I can only vouch for myself. I did what you asked. I did not tell anyone. Honestly, I have no idea who else knows."

"Good."

"Is that significant?"

"It is, and that's why you must keep it private." Tommy Glynn nodded his head in agreement. "The same is true of my next question. Do you know who Jon Silton is?"

"Of course. You told all of us the dead man's name was Jon Silton."

"Did I say anything else about him?"

"He was from out of town. I think you said Sioux Falls."

"Sioux Ridge, not Sioux Falls. What else did I say about him?"

"Nothing. That's when the young gal with the kid began to pass out."

"Do you know what Silton did for a living?"

"Not a clue. He never talked about his work. He never talked, period."

"Did anyone ever say anything about Silton's work?"

"Not to me. Oh, wait a minute, somebody did say he wasn't a truck driver, or maybe they said he wasn't driving a truck."

"Yeah, that's common knowledge." Foneman took a deep breath. "That's all I have. How about you? Any additional information for me?"

"Not off hand." Glynn exhaled a sigh of relief. "I'll let you know if I think of something."

"Fantastic. You confirmed my recollections. Can I count on you to keep our little talk a secret?"

"Certainly, but I have a question for you."

"Go ahead."

"Can you tell me what's going on?"

"Only that I'm not ready to arrest anyone yet. I have some solid suspicions, but no smoking gun. At least, not yet."

"Has to be someone in this building."

"Stands to reason."

"Damn."

"We better return to the storeroom before we're missed. I'll help you carry the beverages. Then I'll sneak back to make a phone call."

* * * * *

"All circuits are busy. Please try again later." Justin Foneman gave up after his fourth attempt to call his office. He had already been away from the storeroom too long. The critical message he wanted to forward to Detective Lorenz would not be delivered. And he would not receive an update on the progress of the army of law enforcement officers descending upon his location. He planted two solid kicks on a plastic trashcan as he stormed out of the kitchen.

Foneman paced up and down the hallway before finally stopping at his two-person table. He pressed down on the tabletop to determine if it would tolerate his weight, and then shoved it back to its previous position partially blocking the doorway of the storeroom, even though he recognized the result of his action might be a missed phone call. Sitting directly on the table, rather than on a chair, would give him a better panorama of the room and its occupants. He also deemed it would make him appear relaxed, which he definitely wasn't, and more imposing than he was.

Oceans of conflicting emotions clashed within the deputy. Elation because he had solved the puzzle and was now watching the killer coolly deal out cards to start a coed poker game. Cracking the case was by far the greatest coup of his entire law enforcement career, and second in his whole life only to capturing the love of the enchanting Stefanie. Anxiety because, not only did he fear for his own well-being, but he did not want to act so foolishly as to allow the perpetrator to escape or take hostages or kill again. One way or another, he knew his name would receive prominent play in newspapers and TV programs throughout Minnesota.

Stay calm, stay calm, he thought to himself. *Don't look directly at the killer. Don't say or do anything to indicate I know the killer's identity. Protect myself and the innocent people in the room. Be careful. The killer may have Jon Silton's gun or another weapon.*

The assassin seemed oblivious to Foneman's clandestine surveillance. Multiple hands of poker were dealt while the female and male players exchanged small talk and good-natured insults. None of them paid attention to the deputy.

Foneman elected not to upset the apple cart. As long as things were going reasonably well, he'd wait until his fellow officers arrived. After he presented his case to Detective Lorenz, they could isolate the suspect and use whatever measures were necessary to make the arrest. He would still be deemed a hero, and, more importantly, he would still be alive.

The decision lifted some of the pressure off his shoulders. He was confident he had fingered the right person, but to be sure, he mentally dissected the evidence and sequence of events again. Everything fit. He couldn't be wrong. But then a simple but neglected fact exploded in his mind like a water balloon hurled from a tall building splattering against the pavement below.

"Holy shit," he said once again, although this time in such a low voice that nobody could detect his frustration.

* * * * *

In his euphoria over identifying Jon Silton's killer, Justin Foneman had made the unsubstantiated assumption that the same person also murdered Father Thomas Pru. Now he was plagued with other thoughts. Silton and Pru had nothing in common, other than they both were almost the same age. Silton was a cop from the southern part of the state, Pru a priest from the northern corner. There had to be some connection between the two if a single killer knocked off both of them.

Once again, Jade Byner was the obvious candidate. She denied knowing Silton, even though they both lived in the same small town. Her dad hired Silton to follow and protect her as she searched for her son's father. Pru was openly friendly to both Jade and Josh Byner, maybe overly so to her little son. And there was the laughing overheard as Jade was allegedly confessing her sins to Pru in a locked room.

No other person had admitted any kind of relationship with Silton. According to all the reports Foneman received, Silton kept to himself. He never initiated a conversation with anyone, except to order food from Margarita. When he did speak, his communications were terse and unwelcoming.

Pru was just the opposite. He was outgoing and managed to have at least short discussions with everyone. He spoke at length with the ghost lady about life after death and appeared to make several attempts to convert Marky to Catholicism. Foneman at one time thought Kelly Nussy might be somehow connected to the priest, but later dismissed the notion when he overheard the young woman's phone conversation and observed her flirting with almost every male at the truck stop except her father. Or was all of that an act?

Foneman had a major problem with further pursuing either Jade or Kelly as the killer of both men. Neither of them was his prime suspect, the person he was convinced shot Jon Silton. He was not ready to concede his error. Perhaps his suspect murdered Pru to divert the investigation to someone else, Jade Byner, for example. Or his suspect could be a psychopath who had no specific reason to snuff out either man. Or there could be two separate killers, each with his or her own motive.

The deranged murderer theory intrigued the deputy. He heard about people who killed for the sake of killing, or to see how it felt to take a life, or for some other crazy reason. Some other crazy reason? Like to communicate with the spirits of the dead. He scanned the room for Lannay Sargetti.

She was sitting by herself, her chair pushed as far away as the tight quarters permitted. Her head was tilted back, her eyes closed. Her lips moved but produced no sound. The deputy couldn't tell if she was in a trance or sleeping or simply resting. She did not look like the murdering type. Too old and too frail to strangle Pru, especially if he was putting up a fight. But he knew that appearances can be deceiving, especially in homicide cases. He felt a sudden urge to use the restroom.

When he returned, Lannay Sargetti waited at his table. "You wanted to talk to me," she said.

"No, I don't. Did someone tell you that?"

"I sensed it."

Foneman pulled a second chair to the table. "You sensed it?"

"Yes, and you're right, you know."

"Right about what?"

"I did not kill the priest."

Foneman's eyes narrowed. "What?"

"I'm too weak to have strangled the priest. Besides, I'm not a violent person. And by the way, my communicating with spirits does not make me a raving maniac."

"I was not . . ."

"Don't bother trying to explain. I know what you were thinking, at least some of it. Let me prove it to you. You already have your man. He tripped himself up. I don't know who he is, but I know you got him."

"I did not arrest anyone."

"I know. He's still there." She bobbed her head toward the storeroom.

Foneman rose to his feet and extended his arm in Sargetti's direction. "Please, walk with me." They strolled down the hall. "How do you do it?"

"Unlike our earlier discussion, this time it is ESP. Extrasensory perception. I can't explain it. I get vibes from angry people. You were upset because you started doubting you had the right man."

"Do you really have ESP?" Foneman was skeptical. The information she had revealed wasn't earth shaking. By now everyone at the Oasis probably guessed he had a suspect or two in mind and assumed Sargetti wasn't on that short list because she lacked the physical strength to strangle a person. And of course the suspect still had to be in the storeroom because no one had left.

"So do you," she said. "How often have you believed you knew what somebody was thinking? Were you right?"

"I can think of a few instances, but that doesn't mean I have ESP."

"Oh, but it does. Everybody has the skill. They just don't accept it or practice it enough to get good at it."

"And you have. Enough to tell what angry people are thinking?"

"Only those in close proximity to me, and I have to free up my mind to be receptive to their thoughts. I don't do that very often. I'd rather use my power to communicate with the dead."

"Have you? With our two deceased men?"

"I feel the presence of their spirits, but we have not communicated."

"Then, they did not tell you who killed them?"

"No."

"So how do you know I have the right man?"

"The force of your own convictions convinced me."

They reached the barricaded door to the fixit garage, turned around, and walked quietly toward the storeroom. Foneman broke the silence.

"I have two questions to ask you. First, will you accept my sincere apology for all my misconceptions about you and the way I treated you? I see now how wrong I was."

Sargetti did not respond immediately. She seemed distracted. "Gladly," she finally said. "I'm always willing to forgive someone who has crossed the line from nonbeliever to believer."

Foneman retained his cynicism, but decided to suspend his disbelief long enough to conduct a brief experiment. If Sargetti really did have supernatural powers, he might as well take advantage of them.

"Will you do me a favor? A huge favor?"

* * * * *

Lannay Sargetti pulled a chair up to the poker game. The four remaining gamblers at the table, anticipating she was about to ask to join the game or say something bizarre, greeted her with inhospitable leers. They were relieved and befuddled when she quietly reclined in her chair and closed her eyes. Dontae Dakota and Marky shifted their eyes to Justin Foneman, catching him staring at them. For three or four seconds their eyes locked. Dakota was the first to look away. Foneman followed a moment later, and the card game resumed without incident.

Foneman tried to spy on the gamblers in the most secretive manner possible. He was watching for one of them in particular to make a telltale or threatening move. He was also waiting for Lannay Sargetti to give him their prearranged signal. Fifteen minutes later it came. Sargetti raised her clasped hands high above her head.

Foneman beamed with excitement as he slipped down the hall into the first sleeping room and waited for the ghost chaser to join him. He was confident all his doubts were about to be dispelled.

"You felt some vibes," he said with certainty.

"No, I couldn't." Sargetti twisted her lips before exhaling a deep breath. "I can't relax enough to clear my mind."

Foneman's face drooped in disappointment. He silently cursed himself for falling ever so briefly for the woman's mumble jumble. He muttered a halfhearted question. "Too nervous to concentrate, are you?"

"No, I'm not a nervous person. I just keep thinking of our last little chat."

"The one in the hallway a few minutes ago?"

"Yes, when you apologized to me. We were walking by the shower room where Father Pru died."

"I remember."

"While you were talking I had this flashback to when I was tending his body. You were comatose on the floor. Sharon Minder came in and lay his Bible next to him. As soon as I saw the book I had an overpowering urge to pick it up. For some reason, I knew I absolutely had to have his Bible. I snatched it while Sharon was covering his corpse with a shower curtain. Now I can't get that scene out of my mind. It repeats itself over and over again."

"What happened after you took the Bible?"

"I never opened it. You woke up. Your eyes were glazed, but I saw them fixate on the Bible. I tried to sneak it out, but Dontae Dakota asked me what I was doing with it. I told him Sharon Minder accidentally left it behind. He volunteered to return it. I couldn't think of a reason to stop him."

"You think the two are related?"

"Dontae and Sharon?"

"No. I'm asking if there's a connection between the urge to take the Bible and the flashbacks?"

"Absolutely, but I don't know the significance. I have a feeling Father Pru's spirit was trying to tell me something about the book."

"Any ideas what?"

"None." Sargetti appeared to be deep in thought as she stared above Foneman's head and slowly rubbed her wrinkled cheeks. "Unless he wanted me to give it to you before somebody else got their hands on it."

Foneman sent Sargetti back to the poker game and then sped to the pantry to retrieve the Bible.

* * * * *

The blue bicycle lock on the pantry door was being obstinate. Justin Foneman's first two nervous attempts to enter the combination ended in failure. The third time he made certain the numbers 1, 0, and 3 were lined up exactly next to each other. The cable pulled apart. He hesitated before entering the pantry, in part due to a haunting premonition that the book would not be there. He was wrong. The Bible was precisely where he had placed it. So were Jon Silton's remains.

Foneman shook the book vigorously, just as he had done before he had locked it in the pantry. The same bookmark and novena card slipped out. He tried to recall Father Pru's last words to him, something like *find the answers in the Bible*. He secured the door with the blue bicycle lock and set off for the storeroom, praying the Bible would provide him with the answers he sought.

Not a sound was coming from the storeroom as he approached it. *Oh geez, now what happened?* Once again, his fear was not fulfilled. Fifteen sets of eyes were watching the door as he entered.

"Where were you?" Ann Nussy's nose flared in fury. "We thought something happened to you."

"Some guard you are," her daughter Kelly added loud enough to cause Josh Byner to abandon his toys and scamper to his mother's arms. "We could have been slaughtered like a herd of old cows."

"Simmer down," the deputy said as he set the Bible down on his table in the doorway. "You're upsetting the boy. I was only gone two or three minutes."

"It would take less than thirty seconds for a psycho to mow us all down," Kelly said.

"Only two or three seconds with an assault rifle," Dontae Dakota said.

"Everyone relax. I'm back now, and my colleagues will be here any minute." Although his last few words were more wishful than factual, they had a settling effect. The heated exchange ended. Josh returned to his toys. Tense postures throughout the room gradually slumped in relief. Foneman thought it was calm enough for him to sit at his table and begin examining the Bible. He hoped what he said was accurate. He hoped his colleagues were almost there.

Searching the Bible was challenging, especially since he didn't know what he was looking for. He first flipped through the pages, pausing to inspect some of the colored illustrations. Then, hoping for divine intervention, he randomly opened the book and read the first two paragraphs on the right-hand page. Divine intervention appeared in the form of Sharon Minder.

"Looking for a certain passage, deputy?"

"In a way. I'm hoping to find something, but I'm not sure what it is."

"That makes it difficult, doesn't it? I read the Bible almost every night. Perhaps I can help if you give me a clue."

"Unfortunately, I don't have a clue to give."

"In that case, remember the advice Father Pru gave me before he passed on to his eternal reward. Go to the Old Testament to soothe your nerves, and the New Testament to seek answers."

After thanking Mrs. Minder for her suggestion, Foneman turned to the table of contents in the front of the book. The Old Testament had almost three times as many pages as the New Testament. He skimmed through the listing of the books in each. Some of those in the Old Testament were unfamiliar to him, but he recognized all of the books in the New Testament. The first was the Acts of the Apostles; the last was Apocalypse, followed by a note in parenthesis, *Also Known as The Book of Revelation*. His eyes focused on the last word. Revelation. If the answer was anywhere in the Bible, wouldn't it be in the Book of Revelation?

He turned to page 1535 and began reading. *Grace and peace be yours from God, who is, who was, and who is to come, and from the seven spirits in front of his throne.*

He continued to the bottom of the page and turned to the next. And there it was. The answer. Written in pencil in Father Pru's own handwriting. The same bullet statements he had seen the priest writing in the margins, three at the top of the page and three at the bottom.

Foneman savored every word in the list.

- Saw the holes in Marky's jacket <u>before</u> he went outside
- Most blood on arm was already dried
- Blood on jacket holes also dry
- Fresh arm wound caused by a cut, not a gun shot
- M too casual for a man who was just shot
- Confronted M, admitted shooting staged, will explain later

The bullets were continued on the next page.

- Confronted M again, refused to answer again
- Told him I thought he killed X.
- Said, gun went off during fight, an accident
- X was a cop, gun belonged to him
- Gun and knife in M's travel bag in booth
- M threw X's stuff in woods behind truck

Another page.

- M didn't want to go to jail
- Told M must confess to sheriff, ask for mercy
- M refused, family needs him
- Told him: 1. He's hurting family
- 2. Would be better for all
- 3. God would forgive

Last page of bullets.

- Gave M one hour to turn self in or I will
- Sheriff watching me, might be on to us
- 30 minutes left, no movement
- Praying for guidance

Justin Foneman felt like he had just been elected Peace Officer of the Year for the entire

United States. Now, thanks to one of the victims, he had Marky for killing a cop and a priest. That ancient aphorism was true. Dead people can speak from the grave. Lannay Sargetti was right.

A cop and a priest. The public will be outraged. In the old days a crazed mob would storm the jail, pull the guilty party from the cell, and exact quick and final vengeance at the end of a rope. No plea bargain, no insanity defense, no never-ending appeals of the verdict, no peaceful natural passing after twenty years on death row. In some respects, the good old days had their merit.

The deputy understood but did not condone Marky's motivation for killing Thomas Pru. The priest was going to turn him in. The murder of Jon Silton was another story. What had the cop done to cause Marky to kill him and then take extreme measures to cover it up, including staging his own shooting and strangling a priest? Maybe the answer to that question was also in the Bible.

"Reading the Bible? The priest must have got to you." Marky's voice jolted Foneman. "A little jumpy, aren't you?"

"I was so involved in the scriptures I didn't see you coming." Foneman closed the book, hoping the man standing before him did not see the handwriting in the margins.

"Interested in a hot game of checkers?"

"Sorry, not now. I committed to watching over everyone. You just proved I was not doing a very good job of it."

Marky's face paled. His eyes moved from Foneman to the Bible and back to Foneman. He took one step backward and watched the deputy's hand inch to the edge of the table above his holster.

"Maybe some other time." Marky retreated into the storeroom, glancing over his shoulder at Foneman.

After witnessing the exchange, Tommy Glynn approached Foneman. "Everything okay?" he whispered.

"No, it isn't. Go into the restaurant and call 9-1-1. If you get through to someone come back and get me."

"Okay," Glynn said loud enough to be overheard by everyone. "I'll get you an aspirin and some ice." A minute later he appeared holding a glass full of ice.

"Ah, just what I needed for my headache."

"No dice with the landline." Glynn's voice was barely audible. "Got a dispatcher named Kadence on my cell. Garbled connection, but she's still there. She tried to tell me something but the only word I could understand was *halfway*. I left the phone on the stove nearest to us."

"Take over my desk while I go to the bathroom. I must have downed too much coffee." Foneman intended for his voice to carry into the storeroom. He started down the hallway toward the restroom but veered into the kitchen, concealing the Bible with his body. The greatest piece of hard evidence in the double homicide had to be stored in a secure location, and he didn't want to raise any questions as to why he was taking the *Word of God* into a bathroom.

The cell phone connection was seventy percent static, but by speaking as loud as he dared and repeating himself multiple times, he was able to convey that Marky was the killer and he could be armed with a gun and a knife. The call cut off before he could confirm the dispatcher understood Marky was not yet in custody and there was no active shooter outside the building. He also couldn't clarify if Detective Lorenz and Sergeant Wyatt were more than halfway or almost halfway to the truck stop.

Justin Foneman grunted in disgust before rejoining Tommy Glynn. "Now I feel better," he said, as though he had just returned from the lavatory. A mild outburst from the storeroom snared his attention.

"Hey, are you listening to me or not?" Dontae Dakota asked loudly. Marky wasn't listening to his monologue about the Iowa towns most likely to have speed traps. He was preoccupied with peeping over Dakota's shoulder to watch Foneman's return. The deputy looked straight at him, ignoring all the other people gathered around the tables. His holster had been moved a few inches forward on his hip, making it more difficult to sit but easier and quicker to remove his weapon. The Bible that had been mesmerizing Foneman minutes earlier was nowhere in sight.

"Sorry," Marky said to Dakota. "I'm not feeling well. My stomach's all knotted up. This tension is finally getting to me."

"I'm a little edgy myself."

"Do you mind if I sit back for a while and contemplate life?"

His contemplation lasted less than ten minutes.

* * * * *

Here it comes, Justin Foneman thought as Marky trotted through the maze of tables and chairs toward him. The deputy remained seated on top of the table. His right hand glided down his side until his fingers made contact with his holster.

"What can I do for you, Mr. Marky?"

"I'm sick. I gotta go to the john." Marky's face was pale and taut with anguish. He looked ill.

"I don't want to let anyone leave the room until my reinforcements get here."

"I can't wait that long. I gotta go now."

"There's a bucket on the shelf in the back corner. You can vomit in that."

"I don't need to vomit. It's the other thing. I feel it's going to blow out any second. Neither of us will like what happens."

"I can't..."

"I gotta go now, and I mean right now." Marky tried to push the table aside so he could pass. He was either actually sick or a very good actor.

"Alright, but I go with you."

"Knock yourself out."

Marky scurried down the hall groaning and clutching his stomach. Foneman, hand resting on the butt of his weapon, followed closer than the sick man's shadow.

"Leave the door open," the deputy said.

"You want the door open?"

"You heard me. Leave it open."

Marky had no time to argue. He yanked his pants down and dropped on the porcelain stool. His bowels broke loose with an explosive sound and a dreadful stench.

"I told you so."

"Yes, you did."

"Can I close the door now?"

"No."

A full minute passed with each man watching the other and saying nothing. Finally, Marky smacked his lips, took a deep breath, looked Foneman in the eyes, and said, "You think I did it, don't you?"

"Did what?"

"Don't play games with me."

"Are you referring to the dead men?"

"Only the one we found in the parking lot. By my truck."

"What about him?"

"Didn't I say no games? I'm trying to have a decent conversation with you and you pull the dumb cop routine."

"Okay, I'm all for a decent conversation. You start."

"I know you think I murdered that man we found by my truck."

"What makes you say that?"

"Oh gee, let's see. Where is your hand? Oh, there it is. On your gun."

"I'd be doing the same for everyone I escort to the lavatory."

"I might believe that if you hadn't changed over the last hour or so. Acting kind of funny around me. You always seem to be watching me. Analyzing what I'm doing. Like you suspect me of something."

"Because I do."

"Well, I haven't done anything wrong."

Foneman paused while he pondered how to respond to Marky's assertion.

Marky was too impatient to wait. "Did you hear what I said? I did not murder that man."

"I heard, but hearing is not believing."

"Believe whatever you want. It doesn't matter. You have absolutely nothing to back it up."

"Actually, I do. In fact, I have more than one piece of evidence that suggests you were involved with Jon Silton's death."

"Suggests? We both know you need more than suggestions to arrest a man."

"I must apologize for my poor choice of words. My evidence does much more than suggest, especially when it's combined with your confession."

"What are you talking about? I haven't confessed to anything."

"Not in so many words, but you might as well have."

"You're nuttier than that ghost lady. Tell me what I said that makes you think I murdered him?"

"You made the classic criminal mistake."

"Which is?"

"You talked too much. Revealed things only the murderer would know."

"I never revealed anything, dude."

"Do you want a few examples?"

"If you actually have some."

"Twice you told me Silton had been shot. Once you even said he had been shot in the neck. How did you know that?"

Marky's only response was a low groan.

"You also said you were going to substitute a terrorist in your book for the dead cop. I never told anybody Silton was a cop. And I got more. But I'll save that for later."

"He told me he was a cop."

"And you conveniently forgot to mention that critical piece of information. In fact, you indicated that you and Silton didn't talk at all."

Foneman and Marky eyed each other without speaking for half a minute.

"Well, Deputy Justin Foneman, you might think you caught me, quite literally, with my pants down. But you are wrong. I said I did not murder the man. I never said I did not kill him. Those are two completely different things."

"Not in my book they aren't, but I'll let that for the county prosecutor to decide. In the interim, I'm putting you under arrest."

"For an accident?"

"Whatever you say may be held against you."

"Might as well, everything I ever wrote has been held against me."

"You have the right to remain silent."

"A little late for that, isn't it?"

"You have the right to an attorney."

"Do you know how many times I've written those same words in my good-for-nothing books?"

"If you can not afford an attorney, one will be appointed for you."

"I know. I know. I waive my rights. I already told you I did it. But I did not intend to kill him. It was an accident. An accident that was his fault. All I wanted was for him to talk to me."

"You killed a man because he wouldn't talk to you?"

"Not exactly, but that's how it started. He was sitting by himself at the restaurant counter last night, so I pulled up next to him. Tried to start a conversation. Thought he wanted to gab for a while. That's why most truckers sit at counters rather than tables. It gets lonely out on that road."

"And he didn't want to talk?"

"Not really, but he didn't tell me to get the hell away."

"So you stayed with him?"

"Yeah, I should've taken the hint. None of this would have happened. Or if he wasn't wearing that stupid sweater. You saw the sweater he had on, the kind that buttons down the front. His wasn't buttoned. I thought they stopped making those sweaters years ago. Anyways, he reached up to put a French fry in his mouth and the sweater pulled away. I saw the holster on his belt. The holster had a badge pinned to it. That's how I knew he was a cop."

"Are you a wanted man?"

"Only by my wife, and then only half the time."

"No warrants?"

"None. I've never committed a crime in my life. All I did was the same thing I did to you. Told him I was a mystery writer with a lot of reject letters because my stories weren't realistic. Asked if he could give me some ideas or read one of my manuscripts and tell me how to make it better. That's all."

"So how did he end up dead?"

"He told me to get lost. Said he was working and didn't want to be bothered. I asked how he could be working at a truck stop in the middle of a blizzard. My question ticked him off. He repeated he was working and told me to scram. Very rudely, I must say."

"And you stayed?"

"No, I left. Kind of pissed, but I didn't say anything or do anything." Marky, still sitting on the toilet, stopped talking.

Foneman waited. When nothing was forthcoming, he said, "I brushed you off, too, but you didn't kill me."

"That's chapter two."

"What happens in chapter two?"

"I had trouble sleeping, so I got up early this morning. Went in to take a shower. Silton was already in there. He must have forgotten to lock the door. His hair was wet and he was getting dressed. He was just about done. I asked if he reconsidered helping me. It was a simple question but he blew up. Used language a cop should never use. Told me what I could do with myself and said he would never help me. Claimed he would put me in jail if I didn't leave him alone."

"Put you in jail? For what?"

"Beats me. I told him he was full of BS."

"And you got into a fight?"

"No. He left and I got into the shower."

"He left. You took a shower. Everything was copasetic. Yet he ended up dead in a heap of snow, and you claimed it was an accident."

"Yes. That's chapter three."

* * * * *

"We're clear on what's going down?" Karen Lorenz was speaking both into the truck's microphone and to the driver in the cab with her.

"Yes, ma'am," the radio answered. The crisp voice belonged to Timothy Barb, the highest-ranking officer in the group slowly progressing toward the target. "You and your deputies will enter the building. My team will do a sweep outside."

"And come inside as soon as you secure the area."

"Yes ma'am. As soon as we determine the status of the shooter and mark everything we find that might be evidence."

"The shooter is the most important. If you stumble across something that could be evidence during your sweep, mark it. Don't feel you have to conduct a comprehensive search in this kind of weather. Last I heard the windchill was a minus thirty."

"Understood. We dressed as best we could for the weather, but we don't want to be out there any longer than necessary. It will be a slow go no matter what. Trudging through snow this deep takes time, especially in the dark."

"Be careful. Don't expose your troops to unnecessary risks, either from the shooter or the weather."

"Don't you think this guy has to be dead if he's been outside all this time?"

"Unless he's in a vehicle with heat. I've been told there are only two tractor trailers and a handful of cars in the parking lot. I'll get the keys for the trucks. Let me know if you need them for the cars. Any questions?"

"How long do we have the snow plows? They might come in handy."

"We're hold on to them for a while. We may need to use their big blades to help capture the shooter. Bullets will bounce off that thick steel as if it were Superman's stomach."

"Oh no we don't." The driver's angry face pivoted to face Lorenz. "Our orders are to drop you off and leave. No mention of sticking around to get shot at. I would never have volunteered for this job if I would have known shooting was involved."

"I can call your supervisor."

"Go ahead. Tell him to come down here and drive the truck himself."

"How about a compromise? Half an hour? Can you wait that long?"

"Ten minutes and no more. Unless guns start going off. Then I'm out of there."

"Ditto for me," the driver of the other truck radioed.

"Fair enough. Do you have anything else, Timothy?"

"No, ma'am," Timothy Barb replied. "We're ready and raring to go."

"Then let's try to speed it up. We need to wrap this thing up quickly, before the interstate opens and hordes of vehicles and people descend upon the truck stop."

* * * * *

Marky gazed at the star shaped badge on Foneman's uniform as though he was hypnotized.

"You all right?" the deputy said.

"I need a drink."

"What would you like?"

"Anything with a lot of alcohol."

"They don't serve liquor here."

"Somebody probably has a bottle or two in their car."

"I'll ask when you finish your story."

"Bribery, huh?"

"If it's the only way I can get to chapter three."

"I'm probably a sucker, but here it goes. Chapter three." He paused a few seconds for effect. "After I dried off from my shower, I put on my ski jacket and cap and went out to check on my truck and get a few things to make my imprisonment here a little more tolerable. I used the back door because it was closest to the truck. Stuck a piece of cardboard by the handle so it wouldn't lock me out."

"Did anyone see you leave?"

"I doubt it. The door to the kitchen was closed. So were all the doors to the sleeping rooms except mine. Even the cop's. I assumed he went back to his room."

"What happened outside?"

"I was moving fast cuz it was so damn cold. My head was down so the wind wouldn't blow in my face so much. The snow was deep, and slippery. I never saw him."

"Silton?"

"Yeah, Silton. He must have gone out to his car for some reason. Or, for all I know, he could have been checking out my rig, searching for a broken taillight or something to hold against me for annoying him in the shower. Anyway I ran into him. Bumped him pretty hard. Didn't knock him down, just sent him reeling. By accident. Didn't even know who it was. At first I thought it was that Dontae fellow checking on his semi."

"Then what?"

"That's when it all hit the fan. Silton must have thought I was attacking him. I wasn't, of course. He backed up a few steps, pulled out his pistol and pointed it at me. Started yelling and swearing. I tried to tell him it was unintentional, but he wouldn't listen. Told me to be quiet and raise my hands."

"Did you?"

"Hands up, yes. The be quiet part, no. I wanted him to know I was going to my truck and wasn't following him. Oh, yeah, he accused me of following him. Can you believe that? Why would I follow a cop? Huh, why?"

"Hard to tell what Silton was thinking."

"He was still fuming when he started coming toward me. Kind of slow like. We were only eight or ten feet apart. Maybe he was going to handcuff me. I don't know. He slipped in the snow and fell to one knee. When his knee hit the ground the gun when off. He shot me. I had my hands in the air, and he shot me. Can you believe that?"

"Sounds like an accident to me."

"An accident that never would have happened if he hadn't pulled his gun in the first place."

"The bullet hit you in the arm, right?"

"Left. It hit the inside of my left arm, a couple inches above the wrist, and skinned my arm all the way up to the elbow. Actually, it was a deep skinning. I was bleeding and it hurt."

"That made you mad."

"Madder than mad. I thought he was going to shoot me again, so I acted on impulse. When he was pushing himself up from the ground I sort of threw myself on him. Tried to knock his gun away, but he was holding it too tightly. Now I was sure he was going to kill me. With one hand I pulled down his jacket, and don't ask me why because I don't know why, maybe because it was all I could manage to do with my bleeding arm. I used my good hand to try to pry the gun away from him. Kneed him in the groin at the same time. His body doubled over, except for his right arm, which I was pulling on while trying to wrestle his gun away. That's when it went off. By accident. I didn't want him to shoot me again. Maybe he pulled the trigger on purpose, thinking the bullet would hit me."

"Silton was shot?"

"Of course he was. You already know that. In his back, by his neck."

"What did you do?"

"Picked up his gun and watched him for a couple minutes while looking around at the same time. I thought somebody might have heard the shot and would come out to see what was going on. Nobody came. Silton sort of stared at me for four or five seconds. Didn't say a word or groan or anything. Then he closed his eyes and mouth and didn't move again. Like he just went to sleep."

"Was he breathing?"

"I'm not sure."

"Why didn't you call 9-1-1 or get help from the people inside?"

"Was going to do both, but panicked as soon as I got in the building. Got angrier and angrier while pressing a towel against my arm to stop the bleeding. That jerk shot me for no reason. At the moment it seemed better not to tell anyone."

"Why?"

"The usual reasons. If he was dead people wouldn't believe my story. Especially you cops. You know how it goes when one of your own kind is killed. One way or another somebody's going to pay big time for it. I figured it was going to be me."

"So you just left him out in the cold?"

"For a short time, maybe fifteen or twenty minutes. Then I went back outside. He looked dead, so I dragged his body to the back of the truck parking lot and took his personal belongings and threw them as far away as I could. Except his money. I kept that. His bullet hole had stopped bleeding. I pulled his jacket collar up to hide the half frozen blood. Then I pushed a lot of snow over his body and buried my tracks. I knew the storm would cover them even more."

"Did you really think you could get away with that?"

"At the time, yes, or I wouldn't have done it. I thought I'd be long gone before he was discovered. My error was I didn't take him to that woody area behind the trucks because the snowdrifts were so high back there. If I had, they wouldn't have found him for days or maybe even weeks. As soon as the girl stumbled into his body I realized how big my mistake was. A little too late then. What was that girl doing where the trucks park anyway?"

"She told me she got turned around in the blowing snow and walked the wrong direction."

"Rotten luck, isn't it?"

"For everybody."

"Where's the towel with your blood on it?"

"In my travel bag. Lucky I always carry an extra shirt and underwear in my bag. I planned to ditch it at a wayside rest stop."

"To dispose of the evidence?"

"Yeah, and that's all you get. I'm done talking." Marky punctuated his statement with a thunderous and stinky deposit.

Both men tried unsuccessfully to stifle their laughter.

"Smells, doesn't it?" Marky said.

"I wasn't going to say anything but it is one of the smelliest stories I have ever heard."

Foneman intended his comment to be witty. He never was very good at humor. His attempt to be funny soared over Marky's head.

"I swear it's the truth."

"Naw, doesn't sound real. Too unrealistic. Just like the books you write." Foneman grinned widely. He might as well have thrown water on a grease fire.

"As if a guy who's been nothing but a sheriff's peon all his life would know."

Marky's remark stung. Foneman's grin evaporated. An evil glare replaced it. "I may be a peon, but I've been around enough criminals to know a phony story when I hear one."

"I'm not a criminal or a murderer. I told you it was an accident. A jury will believe me even if you don't."

"Don't count on it. You better get yourself a darn good lawyer."

"You think I made this up?"

"I don't know. It could have happened that way. Maybe the evidence will be in your favor. It won't be for the second one."

"What second one?"

Foneman glanced down the hall toward the storeroom. All was quiet. Its door was almost closed. No one was in sight.

"Father Pru," he finally replied.

"I didn't snuff the priest. I only killed the other guy. By accident. I had nothing to do with the priest."

"My source told me something different."

"Your source is full of shit, dude. Who is it?"

"Thomas Pru."

"A dead man told you I killed him?"

"You'd be surprised what he told me."

"Such as?"

"You staged the big scene about being shot."

"I was shot. By Silton. I already told you that."

"You were, but long before I got here. I'm talking about when you stepped outside for a moment, pretended to get shot, and fell back into the restaurant. You reopened the wound on your arm with a knife to make it look fresh."

Marky forced an uncomfortable laugh. "I was trying to throw all you cops off the trail so you wouldn't suspect me."

"You used Silton's gun to fire the shot during your little skit."

"To add a touch of that realism I'm supposed to be lacking."

"Father Pru told me the gun and knife you used were in your travel bag. I've confiscated both as evidence."

"Big deal. Neither had anything to do with Pru. He wasn't shot or stabbed. He was strangled with . . ."

"With what?"

"With something. How would I know what? I wasn't there."

"He told me he wanted you to turn yourself in."

"That doesn't prove I killed him."

"He gave you an ultimatum. Either you give yourself up within an hour or he would turn you in."

"When did he tell you all this? That liar promised not to say anything until the hour was up."

"He said that was your motive for killing him. You wanted to avoid going to jail."

Marky sat quietly on the toilet for several seconds contorting his mouth and blinking his eyes before he exhaled a deep breath. "You think you got me, don't you?"

"I do."

"I hate to break it to you, dude, but the only thing you can pin on me is obstructing an investigation. You want to know why? Because I've been lying all along. To you and the priest. To protect somebody. And you would never guess who?"

"One way or another, you are under arrest. Stand up."

"If you arrest me you will be letting the real killer get away. I made up everything I told you. Not one thing is true."

"I have Silton's gun with your fingerprints on it."

"Oh."

"And do you want to bet we will find his other stuff exactly where you said you threw it?"

"I saw somebody toss it in the woods."

"Plastered with fibers from your gloves. And don't forget the bloody towel."

"Well, you're certainly right about one thing."

"What is that?"

"I talk too much."

"Yep."

"It doesn't look good for the home team, does it?"

"Not at all. Stand up."

"Can I wipe myself first?"

"I'll allow you that luxury."

Marky stood facing the deputy. "Do you want to pull up my pants or should I?"

"Pull up your own pants."

* * * * *

The modest daylight that had been visible during the blizzard was long gone, having dissolved into darkness around 4:30 in the afternoon. The wind died down a little but was still blowing waves of loose flakes across the open areas. Those conditions, combined with the weight of the enormous amount of snow they were shoving off Highway 94, hindered the progress of the two state snowplows fighting their way to the truck stop.

Detective Karen Lorenz, perched on the seat next to the driver of the southbound dump truck, strained to see the road over its gigantic curved blade. The SUV driven by Sergeant Wyatt trailed. He was accompanied by a rookie deputy named Billy Joachim, who peppered his supervisor with questions about the role he should play at his first homicide crime scene.

The plow kicked up a thick white cloud as it muscled through the deep snow plastering the highway. The cloud arched over the truck, completely concealing the orange monster with flashing amber lights from the sheriff's vehicle following it. Although it was impossible to be absolutely certain, Wyatt thought he was maintaining a safe distance of nearly a third of a mile behind the plow.

The radio transmission between the two state trucks was amazingly clear. The caravan of police cars following the northbound plow was about five miles from the truck stop.

"How far away are we?" Lorenz said.

"GPS says a little over a mile. You would think it would be more accurate now that the snow has stopped."

"It wasn't accurate before?"

"Hard to tell. We were losing satellite reception on and off."

"Let's hope it's right. Stop here and wait for the team from the south to catch up. We both want to get there at the same time. The greater the force we have, the less the chance the shooter will resist."

The driver stopped his eight-wheeled behemoth in the traffic lane he was clearing and radioed his colleague to notify Lorenz when he reached the one-mile mark. "I hope your guys in the car coming up behind us see we're not moving," he said as an afterthought.

Sergeant Wyatt did see the immobile vehicle ahead, but seeing and stopping were two different things. The SUV slid sideways when he slammed on the brakes, sending the driver's door on a collision course with the rear end of the truck. Wyatt's foot jumped to the gas pedal. The car lurched forward at the last second, missing the plow's back tire by a whisker and smashing into and through the lofty wall of snow the plow had piled on the side of the road. It came to a dead halt fifty feet off the highway.

"Let this be a lesson to you," the sergeant said to the rookie. "Four-wheel drive gives you better traction in the snow, but doesn't do squat for letting you stop better than a regular car."

Despite the truth of his statement about the traction, Wyatt's SUV was mired in such deep snow that he could not make it budge either in forward or reverse. The side doors of the squad car were jammed so tightly against the snow bank that the two deputies could open them only an inch or two. They were forced to scramble over the heap of crime scene gear in the rear compartment to exit through the back gate. Lorenz and the truck driver waited on the freshly plowed portion of the highway for the embarrassed deputies to slog through knee-deep snow.

"You okay?" Lorenz said. The icy air fogged her breath.

"A few bumps, but we survived," Wyatt said.

"You really did it," the driver said. "You're in so far you're going to need a tow to get out."

"How soon can we get one out here?" Lorenz said.

"Not today. The highway has to be cleared better than this for a tow to maneuver enough to pull you out. We're not going to be able get that done until tomorrow morning."

"You can't clear it now?"

"Sure I could, but it would be time consuming and futile. The wind will fill it in with snow before a tow can get out here."

"Not worth the effort," Lorenz said. "We can all fit on your front seat, can't we?"

"It'll be crowded, but it's doable."

"What about the stuff in the car?" Joachim said.

"Take whatever Sergeant Wyatt thinks is important and can be held on our laps. And get something to mark the squad with. It's going to be hard to find once your tracks are covered."

"You mean we have to go back to the SUV?" Joachim said. "I'm already out of breath from traipsing through the snow. Look how wet my pants are."

"Get going, rookie," Wyatt said.

"Let's hurry, guys," Lorenz said. "The posse from the south is getting close."

* * * * *

Deputy Foneman led Marky, his hands cuffed behind his back, into the kitchen. He ordered him to sit on a chair placed against a heavy butcher-block table and cuffed his hands, still behind his back, around one of the table's thick legs. Not escape proof, but it was the best the deputy could do. Marky would have to expend considerable strength and effort to free himself from the table.

"Okay," the prisoner said. "I wasn't lying about everything. What I told you about the cop was true. It was an accident. But I had nothing to do with the priest."

"You're admitting your guilt again?"

"Accidental guilt. For the cop. I didn't kill the priest."

"You had the motive. He was going to turn you in."

"Do you think I'm the only one here with a motive? For a cop, you aren't very observant, are you? He hasn't been exactly getting along with all the people trapped in this place."

"Such as?"

"The ghost lady, and the waitress, and the sassy one whose parents broke up her engagement. Something was going on between him and the girl with the kid, too. And you might as well check out the men while you're at it. Dontae Dakota, for example. He has a violent temper. You saw how he roughed up the ghost lady. That red elastic band he plays with would be perfect for strangling somebody. If you look hard enough you'll find others who had the motive and the means to kill the priest."

Foneman did not immediately react but realized all of Marky's observations were accurate. He removed several knives and a couple meat cleavers from the butcher-block table and placed them in a distant cupboard out of Marky's range of vision.

"I'll get back to you on that," he said at last. "In the mean time you be a good prisoner."

"You be a good deputy and find out who wasted Pru."

Foneman once again repositioned his table and chair in the hallway, this time so he could keep one eye on the storeroom and the other on Marky in the kitchen. He checked his watch. Karen Lorenz's troops were taking longer than he was led to believe. Since Marky had confessed, his plan was to do as little as possible until they arrived. He hoped he would not have to move from his makeshift guard station in the hall.

Margarita Deville appeared in the doorway of the storeroom. "May I come out?"

"You may." Foneman observed a slight hitch in her walk. "You can go by yourself."

"Go where?"

"To the lavatory."

"Oh, that's not why I'm here." She was looking directly at Foneman and did not notice Marky cuffed to the table in the kitchen. "I'm at that age when my legs stiffen up when I sit too long. I need to get up and move around every now and then. That fall on the mustard didn't help very much. Since I'm up I thought I would ask if you might be interested in a bite to eat or something to drink. There's plenty left in the storeroom."

"That's very kind of you, but I'm fine."

"There's nothing I can do for you?"

The deputy hesitated. "Now that you ask." He rose from his chair and moved close to Margarita. "Do you mind if I ask you a personal question?"

"Depends on how personal."

"A few hours ago I observed you in a discussion with Father Pru. He said something that upset you."

"I assume you want to know what he said?"

"I do. I will keep it confidential, as long as it doesn't have anything to do with his death."

Margarita took a step backwards and rubbed her hands together as she mentally composed a response to the question. Her eyes scanned the deputy's face. His expression appeared sincere and caring. She believed he would keep her words private.

"Thirty years ago I had a baby." She spoke in a measured, low voice. "My only child. A son. When he was eighteen we had a big fight in the family. My husband wanted him to join the Marines, just as he did when he was eighteen. My son said he wanted to explore the world. I thought he was too immature to be on his own traipsing around the planet, so I sided with my husband. We told him he could see the world in the Marines or after he completed his enlistment. One Thursday morning in July we got out of bed and he was gone. We never heard from him again."

'I'm sorry to hear that."

"To this day I don't know if he's alive or dead. Back then, I blamed my husband. We argued a lot and got divorced."

Although Foneman felt he knew the answer based on what Tommy Glynn had confided in him earlier, he still asked the question. "What does Father Thomas Pru have to do with your family situation?"

"I've been begging God forever to give me back my son. I thought he had finally granted my wish. Tom Pru's facial features bore a striking resemblance to his father, almost a spitting image. I asked him a few questions about his background and it became all too evident he was not my son. I was disappointed. And sad. I struck out. Again."

"Again?"

"I've done the same thing five or six times since I've been working here with the same result every time."

"Father Pru did nothing wrong?"

"Absolutely not. He was the perfect gentleman. Tried to be very sympathetic to my plight. Even offered to pray for me. It was all me. Watching that little Josh made me miss my own boy so much. I'm so sad. I want my son back."

Foneman's efforts to offer sympathy to Margarita fell flat, so he said he hoped her son would return soon and walked a few steps toward the storeroom with her.

Dontae Dakota stood near the front of the storeroom. The red resistance band was looped behind his neck. He pulled both his arms straight in front of his body, stretching the band to the max.

"Hey, Dontae," Foneman spoke on impulse. "Can I see you for a minute?" Dakota swaggered into the hallway to meet him. The deputy stopped him short of the kitchen door.

"What's up?"

"Does that resistance stuff really work?"

"Sure does. Look at these." Dakota flexed his biceps. "It helps me keep in shape when I'm on the road. Fits in my pocket. I can use it any time, any place. They're indestructible."

"Impressive."

"Try it yourself." He handed the band to Foneman, who stretched it in front of his chest.

"How many of these do you have?"

"Here? Just that one. But you can have it if you want."

"I'll pay you for it."

Dakota laughed. "Not necessary. I can afford a small donation to the local sheriff's department."

"Over-the-road truckers must be paid more than I thought."

"I don't do it for the money. I drive because I like the serenity of the road. Love to be on the open road listening to tunes and watching the scenery. It relieves my stress. I use my owner's prerogative and only take the trips that allow me to hook up with my old friends and biker buddies. Owning a company has its advantageous."

"You really own a whole company, not just one truck?"

"Double D Trucking. At last count, we were up to twenty-seven or twenty-eight rigs. I pay professionals to run the business. I schmooze with the drivers. Talk their language. Take them out for a beer. Act tough sometimes. It makes them feel good. It makes me feel wanted."

"A self-made man."

"A lucky man. I was born and grew up in Montana, but both sets of my grandparents were poor farmers across the border in North Dakota. I inherited land from them. Practically worthless at first. Not much would grow on it. Everything changed a few years ago when they started pumping oil on it. Used the money to buy a firm in Michigan and renamed it Double D."

"For Dontae Dakota."

"Exactly. By the way, that little scrum with Miss Sargetti was mostly a performance. I made absolutely sure I didn't hurt her."

"You could have fooled me."

"Ask her. I apologized to her and we had a good laugh. Now she knows my secret. My biker friends and I are fake wrestlers. We put on impromptu shows, mostly in biker bars. We're pretty good at it. Use noises and exaggerated motions to make it look like we are hurting each other when really we aren't. We fool most people and its good for a few rounds of free beer."

Dakota responded to a series of questions from Foneman about his interactions with Jon Silton and Father Pru. He insisted he never spoke to Silton and his only interface with Pru was an exaggerated reaction to the priest's critique about one of his tattoos.

The priest and the others at the truck stop tended to shy away from him, probably due to his rough appearance and gruff behavior, both of which were invented to protect his introversion around strangers. Kelly Nussy has approached him a couple of times, but he brushed her off quickly. With the sole exception of his apology to Lannay Sargetti, Dakota never involved himself in any meaningful or lengthy conversations with the other strandees, even while playing checkers and poker with them to pass the time.

"What about Marky, your fellow trucker?" Foneman asked. "Didn't you get along with him?"

"Yes and no. We didn't argue or anything like that, but he's not my kind of hauler. Look how he dresses and talks. Too civilized. Too intelligent. Too talkative."

Foneman believed Dakota's story. He thanked him for the resistance band and let him return to the storeroom. The information he learned during the unplanned conversations with Margarita and

Dakota energized him and revitalized his desire to solve the second murder. The pendulum swung the other direction again. To hell with waiting for Detective Lorenz and the others to arrive and steal all the credit and glory.

*****

"Did you discover who did it yet?" Marky said as he watched Deputy Foneman approach.

"Still working on it. Wanted to see if you're doing okay."

"Okay? With my hands behind my back locked to a table heavier than my trailer full of sugar?"

Foneman inspected the handcuffs and the thick leg of the table. Both were secure. "I'll be watching you from the hallway." He carried a chair back to his little table in the hall. After positioning it in such a manner that would not allow whoever was occupying the chair to see Marky without turning around, he ventured into the storeroom in search of his next quarry.

Lannay Sargetti anticipated the invitation. She had been expecting the deputy to ask if she was receiving vibes from anyone, either about what had occurred or was about to happen. Instead, he inquired about the incident with Dontae Dakota. She said she was surprised by the trucker's actions but not harmed and collaborated his story about the apology and laughter.

"No hard feelings," she said. "Dontae's a nice fellow. I'd trust him with my life."

"What about your discussion with Father Pru?"

"We had a debate about life after death. He was adamant. In his opinion, ghosts and spirits did not exist. I begged to differ, of course, but offered a compromise. I've always believed in some kind of life after death, so I conceded there was a heaven. Didn't make a bit of difference to him. He was as stubborn as a rusted nut on an old bolt. Would not consider that some dead people became ghosts before they went to heaven. He walked away from me in mid sentence when he figured I wasn't going to come to his way of thinking."

"Did you try to rekindle the discussion?"

"No. We hardly spoke to each other after that. But do you want to know something else?"

"Of course."

"I haven't had any of those special feelings since you and Marky left the room. Since he never returned, I'm assuming you decided he was the killer."

Foneman glanced over Sargetti at Marky quietly sitting attached to the table. "Let's just say I have him securely tucked away."

"I thought so. I no longer sense another death is imminent."

"I hope you're right about that." The deputy ushered Sargetti back to the storeroom. "Thanks again for all of your help."

He stood motionless in the doorway for several seconds watching Kelly Nussy flit about. Struggling with his building aversion for the young lady, he reluctantly asked her to join him in the hallway in three minutes. Both her parents raised their eyebrows when they heard the invitation, her father out of curiosity, her mother out of concern.

Kelly strutted toward Foneman and plopped down in the chair across the table from him. "I knew you would miss me."

"Miss you? No, but I do have a question or two for you."

"Go for it."

"I noticed you had an unpleasant exchange with Father Pru. Tell me what that was about."

"Not much. He was way too sensitive. I thought a man in his profession was expected to be even keeled and nonjudgmental. He wasn't." She waited for Foneman to respond.

"Too sensitive about what?"

"Do you really want to know? It's kind of personal."

The sudden gleam in Nussy's eyes gave Foneman the impression he was being teased. "Tell me."

"Okay, you asked for it. I merely wanted to know if it were true that some priests have sex with women, especially younger ones. I mean women in their twenties, not teenagers." She paused again.

"And?"

"He blew a gasket. Called me a name I never heard before. Maybe it was something from his precious Bible. Told me I should be ashamed of myself. What kind of a priest would say such a thing?"

Kelly Nussy denied having any additional contact with Pru and volunteered her parents as alibis for the time he was strangled. She described herself as a person who would never hurt a fellow human being, but then added a curious phrase. "At least not physically."

As she rose to leave, Kelly inadvertently turned toward the opposite direction from the storeroom. Marky came into full view.

"What is he doing sitting like that?" she said an octave higher than normal.

Marky answered for himself. "I'm handcuffed to the table. That stupid deputy arrested me for killing both guys. I'm innocent."

"Oh, my God." Nussy plunged back on the chair. "He's the one," she whispered. "I should have known."

"Why should you have known?"

"Because I saw him do something weird a few minutes before Pru was found dead."

"Tell me about it," Foneman said. "But softly. I don't want Marky to hear. Let's move our chairs down the hall. I don't want him to see you either."

Nussy followed the directions but was visibly shaken. "Most of us were in the storeroom when you came in and told us to go in the kitchen for a treat. I started leaving like everybody else, but the strap of my purse caught on a table corner and the whole thing dropped on the floor. Most of the stuff in my purse fell out, so I stooped down to pick it up. When I started to stand I saw Marky all alone in the back of the room. He slipped this long black thing out of his shirt."

"Did you know what it was?"

"Not until I saw the hooks on both ends. It was a bungee cord. Kind of long. Maybe two or three feet."

"What did he do with it?"

"He opened the lid on one of the cardboard boxes that was part of the barricade against the big overhead door. He pulled out a handful of other black bungee cords, put the one that was in his shirt in the box and covered it with the other ones."

"Did he notice you?"

"I don't think so. He never looked in my direction, and I left without saying a word."

"When you returned to the room, did you see him go back to the box again?"

"No, but I wasn't watching him either."

"Can you show me the box?"

"If it hasn't been moved."

The strut in Kelly's gait was replaced with a slow, almost plodding pace. She did not speak until she reached the mishmash of boxes and miscellaneous objects stacked against the loading dock door.

"This one," she said softly while touching the last carton on the shoulder-high stack.

The tan carton was about twice the size of a shoebox. Two square orange and white labels, one pasted on the side and the other on the top, identified its contents. The lid fit snugly but was not taped or otherwise fastened. Foneman lifted the lid with two fingers, doing all he could to avoid smudging any fingerprints that may be on it. The box was half full of black bungee cords. He hypothesized the other half had already made their way into the store to be sold to passing motorists in need of such a device. He carefully replaced the lid and wedged his fingers under the box so he could lift it without contaminating it as evidence.

"I'll be darned," he said under his breath. "This may be the last nail in his coffin."

"But who shot Marky?" Kelly's voice was as soft as Foneman's. "His arm was bleeding."

"Nobody. He cut himself with a knife."

From across the room Ann and Larry Nussy noticed the dramatic change in Kelly's demeanor. They blocked the narrow passageway winding around the tables to the hallway.

"What did you do to our daughter?" Ann Nussy was heated. "Are you accusing her of something?"

"He didn't do anything, mother." Kelly said in a perturbed tone indicative of her embarrassment over Ann's misplaced concern. "We were just talking."

"And a very productive talk it was," Foneman said. "I have other priorities right now, so I must ask all three of you take a seat and let me do my job."

The two older Nussys separated as though they were the waters of the Red Sea parting to allow Moses to pass unscathed. Foneman filed between them, carefully balancing the carton of bungee cords on his way to the kitchen.

* * * * *

"What do you got there?" Marky said as Justin Foneman bypassed him on the way to the pantry.

"As if you don't know."

"I know it's a box. The kind I saw in the storeroom. What's in it?"

"Evidence." The deputy gently set the box on the floor, twisted the tumblers on the bicycle cable lock to 1-0-3, and pulled the cable apart.

Marky watched him carry the carton into the pantry and return empty handed. The pantry door clinked shut. "You're leaving it with the dead guy?" he asked as the deputy locked the door.

"For safe keeping. Until we can run some tests."

"If you're talking about fingerprints, I can save you the trouble. I'm the one who put that box on the stack when we were building the barricade. My prints are on it."

"And on its contents?"

"You can't get fingerprints off rub . . ." Marky caught himself in mid word. He had said too much again. Maybe Foneman hadn't heard him.

"Off rubber? Sure we can. Fingerprints, and even better, DNA. Of anyone who touched it, Father Pru's killer for example. Or of anyone who was touched by it, the deceased priest for example, when he was being strangled." Silence. "You know what we call that in the law enforcement community?"

"No, what?"

"A smoking gun. Have you ever used that term in one of your novels?"

"DNA is not perfect."

"In court it is. The game is over."

"Aw, shit," Marky leaned as far forward in his chair as his restrained hands would allow."

Foneman cracked a slight smile. "Do I take that *aw shit* to be an admission of guilt?"

"Take it to mean get me to a bathroom fast." A loud, stinky fart lent some credence to his demand, although the deputy thought it was somehow engineered for the occasion.

"How did you do that?"

"I'm going to do a whole lot more if I don't get to a bathroom. And I mean right now."

Marky's face twisted in distress as he passed more gas. Foneman decided his prisoner was not faking his discomfort but was uncertain if it was caused by a physical ailment or a wrenching case of culpability accompanied by a foreboding vision of the prison life awaiting him.

"Okay, okay. I'm going to give you the benefit of the doubt. I'll unhook you from the table and take you to the john. But beware. One funny move and the pain you feel will be my bullets ripping your guts apart."

"I mean it, dude. I'm too sick to try anything. I feel like I'm going to explode any second now."

Foneman dropped to one knee, removed the cuff from Marky's left wrist and quickly refastened it behind his back once it was free from the table leg. At the prisoner's urging, they hurried to the restroom in the hallway, the deputy never releasing his grasp on his arm.

"Hurry," Marky said as he stood between the toilet and Foneman. "Make up you're mind. Either unlock my hands or pull down my pants."

*****

Ann Nussy did not waste any time broadcasting to the storeroom's population the salacious bit of unconfirmed news she was able to wrangle out of her listless daughter. Marky was chained to a table in the kitchen. He murdered both men. The pronouncements were met with exclamations of disbelief followed by a tidal wave of relief.

Tommy Glynn was as thrilled as the others to learn that Marky was in custody, but he still harbored a feeling of apprehension. The Oasis manager had been observing Foneman since their dialogue about Silton's death and was concerned for the deputy's safety and emotional wellness. He meandered around the tables to the front of the storeroom and was relieved to see Foneman down the hall, leaning against the wall across from the restroom. He located a spot near the doorway that allowed him to keep a watchful eye on the deputy without being too obvious.

"Where's the sheriff?" Ann Nussy asked in a condescending voice from the side of the room. "Did he leave without us?"

"In the hall," Glynn said. "I can see him from here."

Ann, shadowed by her still lethargic daughter, came forward to see for herself.

"What's he doing down there?"

"Marky's sick. He's with him."

"He should be ill after what he did," Kelly said. "I hope he gets what he deserves."

"We're all sick," Ann said with a snarl. "Sick of sitting around here. They already got their killer. When are they going to let us out?" Her blusterous words prompted a rumble of discontent from the others in the room.

"Yeah, how long do they intend to keep us trapped in this igloo with two dead men and the guy who murdered them?" Sharon Minder said. "Get us out."

"Yes." Ann spoke loudly. "Get us out. Get us out. Get us out."

Almost everyone joined the chant. A few really wanted to go outside, but most were simply blowing off steam now that the most dangerous element of their ordeal was over. Jim Minder was a stoic observer. Josh Byner was so frightened by the clamor that he broke into a high-pitched wail, which silenced the chanters.

Jade Byner lifted her son. "Josh, Josh baby, please be quiet. We'll be home soon. You can sleep in your own bed with your big teddy bear. Or you can sleep with mommy if you want."

"Go home now, mommy," Josh whimpered.

"Soon, Josh, soon. When the storm is over."

"Home?" Margarita said. "Weren't you heading north to find a friend?"

"Not any more. We're going home. My son and I are alive and safe. I need to appreciate the good things I already have in life."

"Talking about leaving," Ann Nussy said, "I want to see what it's like outside. I bet the storm is over and the sheriff is making us stay here because he wants one of us to admit we helped Marky murder those men. I've seen it on TV hundreds of times. The cops put a lot of pressure on people until they confess to a crime they didn't commit."

"You and your TV shows," Glynn said as he entered the room. "That's foolishness." He closed the door leading to the hallway and planted himself in front of it, ready to do whatever he could to prevent anyone from leaving.

"Foolishness, huh?" Ann marched to the barricade blocking the overhead door. "Who wants to see what's happening out there?" She heaved one of the smaller boxes from the barricade against the wall. "Anyone with me?" A slightly larger carton banged off the wall.

Astonished eyes moved between Ann Nussy and Tommy Glynn for several moments as sides were being chosen.

* * * * *

Marky assumed the classic thinker position as he sat silently on the toilet, bent slightly forward, right elbow resting on his thigh, forearm thrust upward, a clenched fist supporting his chin.

"I guess I'm in for it now," he said, his eyes glazed. "I've never hurt a soul in my entire life. Now two men are dead and I killed them. All because of this damn blizzard."

"The blizzard made you kill them?"

"None of this would have happened if I had stayed in Grand Forks instead of trying to beat the storm."

"Yep, but you still are responsible for your actions, storm or no storm."

"I'm going to prison, aren't I?"

"Probably."

"For how long?"

"That's up to the judge. Depends on how cooperative and truthful you are."

"I have been cooperative. I told you about the first one and how it was an accident, didn't I?"

"You did, but what about the second one?"

"It happened almost like you described it. The priest figured out I made up the story about being shot and threatened to turn me in. We argued for a while, but I eventually agreed to give myself up. The shower room was the only spot with some privacy, so we decided to meet there to create sort of a surrender speech. I got cold feet and changed my mind. He said he was leaving to get you and started out the door. I pulled him back. One thing led to another. I went crazy. Next thing I knew my left arm hurt like hell and he was dead."

"Strangled with a bungee cord you just happen to have stolen from a box in the storage room."

"Funny thing about that bungee cord. I took it for him, and, by the way, I was going to pay for it."

"You took the bungee cord for Father Pru?"

"Did you see his belt? The prong on his belt was broken, you know, the long thing that goes in the holes to tighten the belt. He couldn't find a rope or anything to hold up his pants. I remembered the box of bungee cords I saw when I was building the barricade and took one for him. Trying to be nice."

"A thoughtful gesture."

"Once again my nicefulness backfired. He took off his broken belt and tried the bungee cord, but the hook on the end was too big to fit through the loops on his pants. He handed it back to me. Then we started talking and things quickly got out of hand. You know how it ended."

"With a second dead man."

"I did do one good thing for the priest, though. When I was choking him his pants fell down to his knees. I pulled them up before I left."

"I'm sure he appreciated that."

"I'm not as bad as it looks."

"I know."

"Well, that's it in a nutshell. I don't know what else to say."

"I'm sure Detective Lorenz will have more questions for you."

"I'll tell her everything."

Silence.

A deflated Marky stared at the floor, but saw nothing. His mind was numb.

Foneman breathed a sigh of relief. The nightmare was over. He had his man. His hand moved away from his holster. "Looks like you're ready to go back to the kitchen."

Marky knew Justin Foneman was watching him as he reached for the toilet paper. "Could I have a little privacy please? It's humiliating to have someone watch your every move."

"Might as well get use to it." The deputy spoke in a casual voice. He had no idea he was talking to a volcano on the verge of a destructive eruption. "You will really be humiliated in prison. There's no such thing as privacy there."

Marky ground his teeth. Foneman's callousness infuriated him, especially since he had just bared his soul to the deputy. The agitation boiled inside as he rose from the toilet and pulled up his trousers. He fingered his belt buckle without fastening it. *No privacy in prison. Years of humiliation. Perhaps the rest of my life. Rather be dead than go to jail. Make a break for it. So what if I'm killed? I need a weapon. My belt. How fast can I rip it off my pants? Can I get to Foneman before he shoots me?*

Marky's fury was interrupted by an elongated grating sound radiating from the storeroom. Foneman turned his head in the direction of the noise, unaware it was caused by Ann Nussy raising the overhead door. Marky saw his chance. He had to act fast.

Without any forethought, he bull rushed Foneman, jamming the full force of his shoulder into his adversary's stomach. Foneman crashed hard against the wall, and gasping for breath all the way, slowly slid down the wall. By the time he came to rest in a sitting position on the floor, his former prisoner was darting into the kitchen.

Marky headed straight to the blockaded swinging doors leading into the dining area. He heaved the chairs from the barricade in indiscriminate directions, rolled across the remaining table, bashed through the swinging doors, and raced to the booth where he had earlier tossed his outdoor clothing.

As he ran, Marky was struck with a twinge of regret for what he had done to the deputy. It was a stupid, thoughtless act that could not be taken back. The hole he was digging was becoming larger by the minute. The twinge turned into panic as he grappled with his jacket. A finger caught in one of the bullet holes in his sleeve, slowing his progress and eliciting a storm of swear words. He stretched his stocking cap over his head without a problem, but his gloves proved to be another obstacle. His left glove would not fit on his right hand. More cussing. He grabbed his travel bag. The panic had now morphed into uncontrolled terror.

Marky had no escape plan. Primarily because he never thought he would have the opportunity to use one, but also because he felt he would never have the nerve to run from the police. Pure impulse had taken over his life. Why did that damn sheriff's deputy have to look toward the storeroom?

He tramped to the front door and in a rage demolished the small heap of furniture barricading it, re-injuring his left arm in the process. The door balked when he pulled on the handle. After several frantic attempts to muscle his way out he noticed the obvious reason for his failure. The door was locked. A simple twist of the latch knob released the door. He was on his way to freedom.

"Hold it right there." A woozy Justin Foneman stood eighty feet away, clutching his heavy Glock with both hands. "I never killed a man before, but I'm more than willing to do it now."

"Okay." Marky raised his hands, palms facing forward, to be even with his head. A bolt of pain shot through his wounded arm, causing his face to contort in agony. He sucked in two deep breaths. "I didn't mean to hurt you. I wasn't thinking." *Boy was I ever not thinking. I should have taken his gun.*

"You better start thinking now. Because if you move, I shoot."

"Take it easy, man. I got kids. And a wife. I'm not going to try anything."

"Too late. You already have. What were you going to do? That big truck of yours won't be able to get very far with so much snow on the roads."

"It was worth a try. You got here, didn't you?"

Foneman began feeling dizzy. "Hours ago and in a SUV." He took several steps forward, realizing he had to handcuff Marky quickly. The room became hazier with each step. He fought to keep moving, but his legs would not obey. He dropped to his knees. His eyeballs moved upward. *No. Please, not now. Not now.* His gun clanged to the floor. The deputy tumbled forward.

Marky stared at Foneman's prone body until he was reasonably sure the man was unconscious. He lowered his raised hands, picked up his travel bag and opened the door. The wave of cold air assaulting his face made him rethink his flight.

He turned toward the man on the floor, hesitated, and then cautiously approached him. What if Foneman was playing possum, trying to trap him into doing something that would give the deputy justifiable cause to shoot him? Foneman's chest moved up and down, but he appeared to be out for the count. Marky nudged him with his foot. No movement. No response when he called his name. It was decision-making time.

Indecisiveness returned. Suddenly prison didn't seem as bad as it did just a minute earlier. He could wait for Foneman to regain his senses and surrender to him. Or he could take advantage of the situation and flee. He considered his wife and children. Either way he was going to lose his family. At least in prison he would be able to have some contact with them. Unless his wife divorced him and took the kids to California to live with her parents, which he could very easily see her doing. He wavered back and forth between the two options and cursed the blizzard that created such a dilemma.

Giving himself up seemed to be the logical move. Foneman was right. Where would he go and how would he get there? His tractor truck, even if detached from its trailer, would have trouble negotiating the deep snow. A snowmobile or a SUV like Foneman's would not even be a sure bet.

A SUV like Foneman's. Marky froze, his mind gyrating as he reconsidered the options. This would be his last chance. Freedom or a life behind bars? Time was running out. Whichever choice he made would have to be his final decision. There would be no turning back. The pressure was enormous. He wanted to scream.

"Oh, what the hell!" he finally muttered.

He snatched the deputy's gun first and shoved it into his deepest jacket pocket. Kneeling down next to him, he patted the unconscious man's pockets until he found his wallet and car keys. Both slipped out easily. Twenty-seven dollars was all the cash the wallet contained. Flashlights always come in handy, especially the sleek powerful variety attached to Foneman's utility belt, but Marky passed on it. The clock was ticking. He had to hurry. The badge, however, was worth the risk. It might come in handy in the future. He thrust the shiny metal star into the same pocket as the gun.

"I'm leaving now, sucker. No need to get up. See ya." He started to pull himself up. "I changed my mind about that. I hope I never see you again."

* * * * *

Marky hustled to the door. The snow covering the sheriff's car had to be removed before he could make his getaway, and he wanted to get a head start on the other cops, who he assumed would be driving from the county seat up north. He would go the opposite direction. Bracing himself for another surge of frozen air, he pulled his stocking cap down over his ears, and jerked the door open.

"Why hello there," Sergeant Wyatt said. Detective Karen Lorenz and Deputy Billy Joachim stood behind him. "The Mounties have arrived, and believe me, it was not easy."

"Glad you finally made it," Marky said. "Come on in."

The three entered the restaurant stomping the snow off their boots. Marky closed the door and stood behind them.

Almost immediately Wyatt spotted Foneman. "What happened? Why's he on the floor?"

"He's taking a rest, but don't worry. I have his gun, and it's pressed against the pretty lady's head."

The two male deputies turned slightly to verify his statement. "Don't do anything stupid," Wyatt said.

"Don't you do anything stupid. I want you, Mr. Mountie, to walk over to that desk and slowly put your weapon on top of it." Marky kept Lorenz in front of him as a shield. Wyatt silently complied, placing his gun on the hostess desk. "Now walk about thirty feet into the restaurant, but keep your distance from Foneman." Wyatt did what he was told.

Marky ordered Joachim to do the same. His hand trembling, the rookie transferred his gun from its holster to the desk. Marky waited for Joachim to join his sergeant before prodding Lorenz forward. She set her weapon next to the others.

"Open the desk drawer, the big one on the right," Marky said. Lorenz pulled the drawer open. "Pick up each gun by the barrel and put it in the drawer. No funny business or you're dead."

"Are you sure you want to do this?" Lorenz said.

"Of course I'm sure." He raised his hand holding the gun as though he was going to strike her with it.

"Don't do anything stupid."

"Don't do anything stupid," he shouted. "You cops like saying that, don't you? It's your catch phrase. Well, you're right, sweetie. You convinced me. I won't do anything stupid. Why waste all this firepower? Four guns are always better than one."

One by one Marky jammed the barrel of each of the pistols under his waistband, allowing their grips to protrude above his waist. He hip checked the drawer shut and marched the detective to where the two deputies were waiting.

"Now listen to me carefully. If you don't do what I say and in the manner I tell you to do it, there will be cop blood all over this restaurant. The first thing you're going to do is be quiet. You keep your mouth shut unless I ask you a question. Everyone understand that?"

The three captives nodded their heads, the rookie with a terrified expression, the other two pokerfaced.

Marky pointed at Billy Joachim. "You, how many pairs of handcuffs do you have?"

"One."

"Okay. Put your bracelets on the big guy with the stripes. Behind his back, not in front." He watched Joachim put the restraints on Wyatt. "Now take his cuffs and put them on the lady here, and then get hers."

"Mine are in my fanny pack."

"Did I ask you to talk?" Marky slapped Lorenz on the side of the head.

"I'm trying to help you."

"I don't need your help. All I need you to do is be quiet. Your yapping makes me nervous, and believe me, you don't want to make me nervous. Understand?"

Lorenz bobbed her head in agreement. As Joachim extracted the contents of the fanny pack the detective exchanged glances with Wyatt. Their eyes darted up and down and sidewise, but their attempts to communicate with each other failed.

"Give me the money." Marky pocketed the small wad of one, five and ten dollar bills that had been in the fanny pack. "You might as well give me yours, too." Joachim handed over the cash in his wallet. "And the big guy's." Wyatt's billfold was packed with four hundred dollars worth of twenty-dollar bills he had withdrawn from an ATM Saturday morning. "Wow, the mother load."

Marky ordered the rookie to use Lorenz's handcuffs on Deputy Foneman, warning him not to do anything to revive the comatose man.

"How is he?" Karen Lorenz asked, risking severe repercussions from her captor.

Joachim looked up from his kneeling position to gauge Marky's reaction.

"Tell her," he screamed at the deputy.

"He's not dead. Other than that I don't know. I don't see any wounds or blood."

"That's because there aren't any." Marky turned away from Joachim and took two steps toward Lorenz. "He dropped over on his own. Did the same thing this afternoon. I had nothing to do with either of them."

"Good," Lorenz said. "We won't have to charge you with assaulting a police officer."

Marky moved to within a few inches of the detective. A sneer warped his face. "It's time for you to shut up again, Missy, or you will never be charging anyone with anything ever, ever again." His spittle splattered against her cheek.

Lorenz held her ground, battling to conceal her rage and fear.

"Do you want his money?" Joachim said in an effort to divert Marky's attention away from Lorenz.

"Don't bother. I already cleaned him out. And got his handcuffs."

"I have them."

"What?" Marky glimpsed a set of cuffs in Joachim's hand. "Look at that. He had a second set. Bring them over here."

Marky snapped the last pair of handcuffs on Joachim before directing his three prisoners to walk through the kitchen. He followed with the tip of the Glock pressed against Karen Lorenz's upper spine. "I'm surprised," he said. "Only three of you showed up. The way your pal was carrying on, I expected to see an entire army of cops, not three inept sheriffs."

"We're a small department," Wyatt said. "Most of our deputies couldn't make it into the office because of the blizzard."

"But you made it here."

"We did."

"In a SUV?"

"Yes."

"Your car must be nice and warm and free of snow."

"It is."

"Where is it?"

"A few feet from the door we came in."

"Where are the keys?"

"In the ignition."

"They better be."

The group moved into the hallway behind the kitchen and stopped in front of the closed door leading to the storeroom.

"I want you to meet some of my friends," Marky said. "You will be spending a little time with them. Open the door."

"How?" Wyatt said.

"Not too bright, are you? Your hands are locked behind your back but they still work. Back up against the door and grab the handle."

The storeroom was a disastrous scene. All the cartons and other objects once used to barricade the overhead door were strewn around the room. Some of the chairs were tipped over, as was the small table Foneman had been using. Only the

Minders and Jade Byner and her son were sitting. The others were milling about in various stages of irritation and frustration waiting for Foneman to return. The movement came to an abrupt halt when the door opened. All eyes focused on the three newcomers and the truck driver behind them.

"We have company." Marky emitted an evil chuckle. The handcuffed wrists and the gun pressed against the female detective were plainly visible.

The occupants of the storeroom were overcome with shock. Even four-year-old Josh Byner was quiet. Thanks to the absolute silence, the soft-spoken words of a slow moving figure sneaking behind Marky were audible to everyone.

"As a famous cop once said, go ahead, make my day." The voice belonged to Deputy Justin Foneman.

Marky felt a cylinder-shaped metal object press against the back of his head. "You're full of it. You don't have a gun."

"What do you think this is?" He poked Marky's head with the object.

"Not your gun. I'm holding your gun against this fine lady's back. It's probably your damn flashlight."

"Where's your bag, Marky?"

"Don't know and don't care."

"You left it next to me on the floor. Remember what was in it?" The words were uttered slowly and in a taunting tone. "Jon Silton's gun. It's loaded and the safety is off. Ready to split your brain wide open."

"You told me the gun wasn't in the bag any more."

"I lied."

"You're lying now."

"It's a Smith and Wesson. One of those new lightweight models. Might not even recoil when I shoot someone in the head. What do you think? Should I give it a try?"

Marky wavered. The dead cop's weapon was a lightweight Smith and Wesson. "You're too smart for that. You pull the trigger, my reflexes pull my trigger. You know what that means. You don't want to see your lady friend dead, do you? The home team wins this one, deputy. Put the gun on the floor."

"Wrong, Marky. Your team loses again. She's not my friend. I hate her. Always have. You'd be doing me a favor. She's been trying to get me fired for years. I get rid of two birds with one bullet. You and the bitch. Your choice. But you better hurry. I'm getting dizzy again. I might accidentally put a bullet in your head."

"Foneman, you bastard." Karen Lorenz's voice was frantic. "I should have taken you down years ago, you spineless pig. I hope you rot in hell."

"Crap." Marky exhaled disgustedly and pointed the gun to the floor.

"I'll take that." Foneman seized his Glock and stuffed it in his holster.

"He has three more under his belt," Karen Lorenz said as she turned to face her adversary.

"Hands high." Foneman demanded. "Mr. Glynn, would you kindly relieve this gentleman of the three firearms and place them on the floor behind me."

"My pleasure." Glynn grinned at Marky as he removed each weapon.

"Now, Mr. Mystery Writer," Foneman said, "lean against the wall and spread your legs." No other weapons were found during a pat down.

"I should have let you shoot me," Marky said. "Might as well be dead. Not much to look forward to now, is there? And I would have done you a favor. Taken care of the lady cop for you."

"I lied about that, too. We're the best of friends."

"Figures."

"Hands behind your back."

"How did you do it?" Marky asked as he was being handcuffed.

"Do what?"

"Get out of those bracelets?"

Foneman threw him a puzzled look.

"I never locked them," Billy Joachim said. "I placed them over his hands but never shut them. You were too distracted to notice."

"A young genius," Lorenz said.

As if on cue, the miniature radios clipped to the shirts of the two deputies crackled to life. "Fresh foot prints on the loading dock in the rear of the building," a muffled voice said. "Two sets.

Smallish. Could be women. They didn't go very far. Looks like they came out and went back in."

"Who's out there?" Foneman said.

Karen Lorenz, her lips curled in a victory grin, maneuvered to be face-to-face with Marky. "The army of cops this guy wanted."

"We can call them off. There is no shooter. Marky did it all. Even intentionally shot himself."

Foneman had Marky sit on the floor a safe distance from the weapons of the officers. He turned on the radio clipped to his own shirt that he had deactivated hours earlier because he was bothered by the constant static. The searchers were relieved to learn an active shooter did not exist and delighted to hear Detective Lorenz's voice in the background instructing them to abandon the frigid outdoors in favor of the warm restaurant.

As Deputy Foneman freed his colleagues from their restraints, the strandees in the storeroom who witnessed the drama unfold in stunned silence now jabbered in excitement. Foneman shouted above the racket. "Listen, folks. I'm going to shut the door for a few minutes. There is absolutely nothing to worry about. You are all safe now. There are lots of officers here and we have the culprit." The announcement was greeted with a resounding cheer.

"So the idiot who had a gun in my back is Marky?" Lorenz said.

"One and the same."

"And he shot himself?"

"Did I say that? I really meant to say he staged a shooting to make it look like another party shot him. And, by the way, he confessed to both murders."

"The first one wasn't murder," Marky bellowed. "It was an accident."

"We'll take that into consideration," Lorenz said. "Did you read him his rights?"

"He did," Marky answered for Foneman. "I told him I don't want an attorney."

"Let's take a walk," Foneman said to Lorenz. They headed down the hallway. "He confessed to both murders after I read him his rights. But then he said he was lying about the dead cop and covering up for someone. Then he waffled back the other direction and said he did it again."

"What do you think?"

"Guilty of both. Maybe the first one was an accident, but I doubt it. You'll see for yourself when I tell you the whole story and give you the proof. They're solid cases."

"Mr. Mark Key," she said upon returning to the threesome at the end of the hall. "I understand what you told me. To assure there is no confusion or misunderstanding, I want to tell you why we are arresting you and read you your rights once more. This time while I'm recording it on my smart phone in front of these three witnesses."

"Whatever."

The repeat of the Miranda warning elicited the same response from Marky as he had given Foneman almost an hour earlier. "I don't need an attorney. I admit I did it, including assaulting the deputy. I'm guilty of everything. Except the first one was sort of an accident."

The detective told Deputy Joachim to take the prisoner to the last sleeping room and watch him like a hawk. She wanted to question him soon, before he changed his mind about the lawyer and the confessions. First, however, she needed to hear Justin Foneman's narrative of what had transpired at the truck stop. Viewing the bodies could wait. They weren't going anywhere.

At first she intended to continue the isolation of the witnesses in the cramped storeroom. Then she realized they had been together for so many hours in such a tight space that cross-pollination of their stories had already taken place. Their memories and testimonies would be influenced by what they heard others say and do. Increasing the isolation would likely lead to more cross-pollination. After a brief lecture about what they could and could not discuss, she released them to return to the dining room. From the sounds already coming from that area, she deduced they would be joining the law enforcement officers already there warming their cold bodies.

Justin Foneman suggested they move to the administrative office near the front door, but Lorenz wanted to remain in the storeroom so she could keep an eye on the young deputy guarding the double murderer. With the door wide open, Detective Lorenz and Sergeant Wyatt positioned their chairs so they could see Joachim's station down the hall. Across the table sat Foneman. They listened intently to his narrative.

* * * * *

"I have an update," Detective Karen Lorenz announced to the crowd in the restaurant at 11:56 p.m. "The wind is blowing itself out. The temperature is still only eight degrees above zero, but it feels a lot warmer without the windchill. And, of course, the snow stopped falling several hours ago. I am officially declaring this blizzard to be over."

The declaration drew applause and cheers from both the trapped travelers and the peace officers, all of whom were too wound up with excitement to sleep. Kelly Nussy jumped to her feet, apologized for her off-key singing voice, and parodied a verse from the movie *The Wizard of Oz*. "Ding, dong the blizzard is dead. The wicked blizzard, the wicked blizzard. Ding, dong the wicked blizzard is dead." The audience laughed and clapped.

"I've spoken to MnDOT," Lorenz continued. "They anticipate the interstate will be open in both directions around nine tomorrow morning. I've been told officers have almost completed interviews with all of you and you have been informed you may be contacted again in the future and may be called as witnesses. Therefore, with one exception, you are free to go as soon as the highway is drivable."

"I can guess who that exception is," said Ann Nussy.

"I stated that incorrectly. I should have said two exceptions. You know about the first one. The second is Dontae Dakota." Lorenz paused. Dakota flinched. "He did nothing wrong. The reason he can't leave is because the truck parking lot is a crime scene. The state crime investigators will not arrive until late morning and it will take a fair amount of time to process the scene. Actually, I don't know how they're going to manage that chore with a couple feet of snow covering everything."

"You mean I may have to stay here an extra day?" Dakota said.

"Your eighteen wheeler has to stay here. We'll put you up in a nearby hotel and foot your expenses."

"I can taste the lobster now."

"Reasonable expenses. None of you will be allowed to go to the truck parking lot. Once you leave, the entire truck stop will be closed for a few days because it also is a crime scene. Some of the officers in this room will help cordon off the area and assist in other ways in the investigation."

"We heard that Marky confessed to killing both people," Sharon Minder said.

"I understand such a rumor started because two curious women, who just happen to be related to each other, had their ears pressed against the door of the storeroom while we were questioning the suspect in the hallway. At this time it is simply a rumor. I can neither confirm nor deny any statements by Mark Key or any other person."

"Are you looking for another person?"

"No, we are not."

Larry Nussy rose. "I would like to say something. I would like to commend Deputy Justin Foneman for what he did down here today. He single-handedly managed a very tough situation, kept us in line, and caught the killer. I think the county owes him a huge raise and a medal."

Ann Nussy stood up and began clapping to honor her former opponent. Within a few seconds everyone, including the law enforcement personnel, were on their feet cheering and clapping. An embarrassed Justin Foneman thanked everybody and said he couldn't have done it without their help. He gave special mention to Tommy Glynn and Lannay Sargetti. The reference to Glynn surprised no one. He had frequently been observed assisting the deputy. Sargetti's name was a shocker. How could that kook have helped the deputy? He always had appeared to be exasperated with her. The connection was not divulged.

The three deputies returned to the storeroom to complete the incident debriefing in private.

"I never received a standing ovation," Sergeant Wyatt said. "Or a sitting ovation for that matter."

"And no one ever said I should get a raise and have a medal pinned on me," Detective Lorenz said.

Foneman blushed. "They're not being objective. They're delirious because this big mess is over. I'm not a hero. I really screwed up. Passed out when the pressure was on. Not once. Twice. Almost three times. Worst of all, the priest was killed on my watch."

"I beg to differ," Lorenz said. "You're my hero. I might be dead right now if it weren't for you."

"We all might be," Wyatt said. "Nothing worse than a perp in a panic mode and loaded with firepower."

"Given the conditions foisted upon you, your performance was exemplary. You were all alone here during a blizzard. Communication with the outside world was intermittent and unreliable. Plus you had a group of angry, scared people on your hands."

"And don't forget one killer," Wyatt added, "who you identified and apprehended."

"He, by the way, confessed to everything in short order," Lorenz said. He strangled Pru with a bungee cord from the storeroom and returned it there after the crime. He even showed us where the carton had been. He did change his story about Silton, however, but still claims it was an accident."

"The gun didn't go off in a struggle?" Foneman said.

"That remains the same. So does the part about Silton blowing up when Marky bumped into him. What's different is that Silton didn't draw his weapon until Marky threatened to tell Jade Byner he was watching her. He thought the threat would make Silton cool the rhetoric, but it had the opposite effect."

"How did he know Silton was tailing Byner?"

"Deduced it. Noticed Silton was continually glancing over at her in the restaurant."

"Are you buying that story?"

"At least for the time being," Lorenz said. "The medical examiner will look at the entry angle of the bullet to determine if it jives with Marky's story. The ME should also be able to tell us if Silton died instantly from the gunshot wound or if he succumbed to the wintry elements after Marky left him outside unattended."

"Nevertheless," Wyatt said, "it was a good confession. We recorded him on video and now he's writing everything down on paper. Thanks to you, we got our man."

"I still don't feel good about it. How could I have talked to Marky several times before he faked his shooting and not noticed the two bullet holes in his shirt?"

"Because they weren't there," Lorenz said. "He changed to a nearly identical shirt after Silton shot him so nobody would ask questions. Then he switched back again before going outside for the big charade."

"Even so, I should have done so many things differently."

"I feel the same way with every case I have ever worked," Lorenz said. "Look at it this way, you accomplished the major things cops are told to do at a crime scene. You protected yourself and the other people trapped here. You did your best to secure the area from contamination. You identified suspects, narrowed it down to one, and arrested the perpetrator while he was threatening to kill three fellow officers. What else can we expect?"

"If anyone deserves a raise and a medal, it's you," Wyatt said.

"I just want to go home and see my wife Stefanie and go to bed. I'm so tired."

"I will guarantee you will be the first one out of here."

AFTER THE BLIZZARD

Tommy Glynn was awarded a $35,000 bonus by the owner of the Midway Truck and Traveler Oasis for going beyond the call of duty during the blizzard and ensuing crisis. He hopes to purchase the business when the owner sells it next year.

Jade Byner vowed she would live her life to the fullest. She terminated her search for Josh's father and repaired the damaged relationship with her parents.

Dontae Dakota won the semi truck driver rodeo in Michigan and placed third in the national competition. His company, Double D Trucking, continues to expand. He plans to return to Sturgis, South Dakota for next year's motorcycle rally.

Lannay Sargetti still claims to feel vibes from angry or deceased people. Despite multiple attempts, she has never encounter a ghost. Her role in the investigation of the murders was never revealed to the public.

Small talk over breakfast at the Truck and Traveler Oasis restaurant between **Kelly Nussy** and **Deputy Billy Joachim** led to a serious relationship. Together they moved into a house in a town twenty-three miles east of the truck stop. They are expecting twin girls in three months.

Two weeks after the blizzard, **Margarita Deville** and **Chevy Mato** were struck by a drunk driver in a pickup truck as they walked to Deville's vehicle in the parking lot of the Oasis. Deville was seriously injured but returned to work after ten weeks of physical therapy. Mato died at the scene.

Allie and **Jager Rellik** were unaware their last name spelled backwards was killer. Neither were Jager's parents nor grandparents. Allie and Jager are both well on their way to success in their chosen careers.

Sharon and **Jim Minder** and **Ann and Larry Nussy** returned to their homes with the goal of living happily ever after. So far, so good.

Marky Key pled guilty to one count of manslaughter and one count of homicide in the second degree. He is currently serving a forty-year sentence in state prison.

National media hailed **Justin Foneman** as a hero and the county awarded him a distinguished service medal. Due to his health issues, however, he was removed from active patrol, but a new position of Community Liaison Deputy was created for him. He and his wife Stefanie coauthored a book about the ordeal at the truck stop using the penname Michael Lorinser.

CPSIA information can be obtained
at www.ICGtesting.com
Printed in the USA
FFOW03n1301181215
19507FF